Through the w... broad shoulder... A starkly mascu...

Tired, shaking, she fou... ...n panic. She drew a ragged breath and squeezed her eyes shut against the dull ache in her head. 'Please,' she begged. 'I'm cold. So cold.'

'Come in,' the man said gruffly.

She hesitated. Took another look at the stranger. If only she could see a glimpse of a smile.

But the cold drove her into his cabin. And she shivered again.

Outside, she'd craved only escape from the storm.

Now she wondered if she was safe.

If only she knew where she was. If only she knew this man.

If only she knew her name...

Dear Reader,

A new year and it's going to be a really dynamite year for Silhouette Special Edition®, too! It's starting off with Susan Mallery's THAT SPECIAL WOMAN! title where the story is also linked to her HOMETOWN HEARTBREAKER mini-series. So make sure you take a look at *Husband by the Hour*; as always, it stands alone, but if you've read Susan's previous books, you'll no doubt be pleased to revisit old friends.

Victoria Pade returns with a new Heller family story, *Cowboy's Lady*, where Ivey actually runs away from her own wedding...! Jennifer Mikels delivers a classic amnesia story, *Remember Me?*, and Ruth Wind gives us a secret baby book, *Marriage Material*, in the first of her FORREST BROTHERS novels—look for the next one in Silhouette Sensation® next month.

Welcome newcomer Barbara Benedict to the Special Edition™ list and sit back and enjoy her *Rings, Roses...and Romance*, it's got a gorgeous single father, irrepressible kids *and* an Antebellum mansion in the deep South.

Finally, *New York Times* bestselling author Ellen Tanner Marsh takes one millionaire who's a confirmed bachelor and one ordinary girl, puts them together, stirs them up with a healthy dash of attraction, and soon that high-powered man doesn't know if he's coming or going!

Enjoy them all,

The Editors

Remember Me?

JENNIFER MIKELS

SILHOUETTE

SPECIAL EDITION

Silhouette, Silhouette Special Edition and Colophon are
registered trademarks of Harlequin Books S.A., used under licence.

First published in Great Britain 1998
Silhouette Books, Eton House, 18-24 Paradise Road,
Richmond, Surrey TW9 1SR

© Suzanne Kuhlin 1997

ISBN 0 373 24107 0

23-9801

Printed and bound in Great Britain
by Mackays of Chatham PLC, Chatham

JENNIFER MIKELS

started out an avid fan of historical novels, which eventually led her to contemporary romances, which in turn led her to try penning her own novels. She quickly found she preferred romantic fiction with its happy endings to the technical writing she'd done for a public relations firm. Between writing and raising two boys, the Phoenix-based author has little time left for hobbies, though she does enjoy cross-country skiing and antique shopping with her husband.

Other novels by Jennifer Mikels

Silhouette Special Edition®

A Sporting Affair
Whirlwind
Remember the Daffodils
Double Identity
Stargazer
Freedom's Just Another Word
A Real Charmer
A Job for Jack
Your Child, My Child
Denver's Lady
Jake Ryker's Back in Town
Sara's Father
Child of Mine
Expecting: Baby

Chapter One

Where was she? Pushing back her dripping hair, she squinted through the blurry mantle of rain. She'd been running through the woods for so long that her side ached. She needed to rest but was afraid to, for if she stopped, she'd have to think.

Slippery, the ground played the enemy. Twice she fell to her knees. She couldn't remember where she'd started running. Only when.

A flash of lightning had eerily illuminated the woods. Thunder had rumbled deafeningly and panic had surged through her, not from fear of the storm but from the emptiness in her mind.

After scrambling to her feet again, she clamped her mouth tight to keep her teeth from chattering and pushed away brush to reach the clearing beyond trees. In staggering steps, she plodded through the mud then saw the outline of a cabin, smoke drifting from the chimney.

Maybe she had come from this cabin, wandered outside. Then what? She'd fallen and hit her head?

Exhausted, she lunged for the cabin stairs. What if she'd been running from someone inside? She fought dizziness and leaned against the cabin door, unsure about entering. None of that might be true, and she wanted warmth, dryness. She wanted to close her eyes.

Inside the cabin, Nick Vincetti poked at the fire he'd started moments ago. Steadily rain fell, coming down in a syncopated beat on the cabin roof as a November storm brewed with a vengeance.

He sipped at lukewarm coffee that he'd poured from a thermos. Though tired from driving to the cabin, he was in no hurry for bed. He'd left schedules behind him in Chicago. One perp was in jail, awaiting trial. Another investigation was stalled by a lawyer who claimed police had harassed his client. Forget all of them. For two weeks he would put trouble behind him.

His stomach rumbled, reminding him that he hadn't eaten since noon. He yawned and snatched up his jacket, sliding it on while he strode to the door to haul in the last two cartons. One of them contained a loaf of bread and a jar of peanut butter.

As he stepped off the porch, mud sucked at his boots and buried one foot to the ankle. Looking down with an oath, he gave his foot a shake. He took two strides forward, then stilled, alert to banging from the back of the cabin. Drenched already, he squinted against the rain and followed the sound to the back door.

Darkness shadowed the stairs, but he caught movement. A dark figure stood by the door—a woman, he decided instantly. Hair dripping and coated with mud, she clung to the door, her hand gripping the doorknob. Lightning revealed a face that looked pale. "Lady, what are you doing out here?" he yelled to be heard over the howl of the wind.

As she whipped around, the beam of a flashlight glared at her. She blinked hard. He'd called her "lady," she reminded herself, amazed her brain managed such a rational thought. She shrank against the door, even when he lowered the flashlight, no longer blinding her. To see him more clearly, she wiped a hand across her damp face.

He hunched broad shoulders as rain battered at him. She noted slashing cheekbones, a strong, masculine face. His dark hair was shaggy, overlong and ruffled by the wind. He kept staring at her as if she were crazy. Did she look that way? She drew a ragged breath and squeezed her eyes at the dull ache in her head. Tired, shaking, she fought panic. If she had a few minutes from the wetness and noise of the storm, she could think clearly. "Please," she nearly begged. The wind masked her voice as she hugged herself. "I'm cold. So cold."

Cold and wet himself, Nick saw no point in both of them freezing while he got answers. "Go in."

She wanted to but hesitated and sneaked another

look. If only she could see his face, a glimpse of a smile.

Trembling with cold, she scurried into the cabin. As she passed through a short narrow hall, she touched a closed door to what she assumed was a bedroom. The thought of a bed tempted her, but she kept moving toward the warmth of the fireplace. Though dry, the cabin held a chill, and she shivered again. Outside, she'd craved escape from the cold. It was all she'd thought about when she'd seen him. Now she wondered if she was safe. If only she knew where she was. If only she knew her name.

Nick jammed his hands into the pockets of his parka and stalled for a minute, trying to judge the situation. When he'd neared the back of the cabin, he wasn't sure what he'd expected, but it hadn't been some woman looking half-drowned. As she'd opened the door, he'd noted apprehension in her face. Because she'd looked scared, for her peace of mind, he'd maintained his distance until she'd stepped inside.

Rain beat at him, but he took the time to scan the dark woods surrounding the cabin. He had to consider the possibility that someone was chasing her... perhaps an irate husband or abusive boyfriend with a cockeyed notion that she belonged to him.

Some idiot bursting into the cabin didn't worry him. For the past twelve years, even when in uniform, he'd dealt with the dregs of society. But he'd left the city, hoping for a brief respite from them.

Trudging through the mud, he resigned himself to no solitude, no peaceful two weeks in an isolated cabin to forget a homicide that had kept him hopping for nearly a year. Instead he had unexpected company.

At the door, he pried off his boots then entered the one big room containing the fireplace. He found her shaking, facing the fire. Her clothes hid little, since she wore no jacket, and the soaked white sweater and snug jeans clung to her.

Thin and tall, nearly five foot eight, she was dirty, but he gathered impressions. She had high cheekbones, a thin nose and generous mouth, a look that denoted good breeding.

With his step forward, she skittered halfway to the door. "Take it easy." He rummaged in a carton for two towels and tossed one onto a chair near her while he dragged the other one over his face. Without looking at her, he lifted an extra blanket from another carton and draped it over a chair. As if her arm weighed too much, she raised it slowly and touched her forehead. Nick eyed the small bump just to the right of her eyebrow. "You're hurt. Did you pass out?" he asked while digging into his duffel bag for a bottle of aspirin.

"No." She spoke so softly that he got the answer by lipreading.

"Are you nauseated?" he asked, trying to eliminate a concussion. If she went into shock, he'd be in a hell of a fix traveling over rain-soaked, rutted dirt roads to get her medical care.

"I'm just cold," she said in a stronger voice, and snapped up the blanket to drape it around her shoulders.

Nick scratched off one problem while he palmed the aspirin bottle. "Why don't you sit by the fire?"

Still warily keeping an eye on him, she moved on command, slowly.

He couldn't offer much in the way of a reassurance. He thought of himself as one of the good guys. Even with women he'd dated then stopped seeing, he'd made sure the relationships had ended without animosity. For now, until she felt more comfortable around him, he'd keep his distance. "Did you have an accident?"

Don't ask me too many questions, she wanted to say. "Is there anyone else here?"

Nick didn't miss the nervousness in her voice. "No, there isn't."

"You aren't married?" As he intently watched her, she gathered the blanket tighter. She wished for the company of a woman, for someone who might understand the helplessness overwhelming her. She wished she didn't feel so scared.

"Not anymore," Nick answered. Lightning slashed across the sky. Rain hammered harder. While he banished a quick image of his ex-wife, he peeled off his wet parka, then hung it over the back of a chair.

"Where are we?"

"Near Rhinelander." Tired from driving, he decided to get facts, then show her to the bedroom. In the morning, he would deal with his next problem…getting her wherever she'd been going. He turned and took one step toward her with the bottle of aspirin. "Do you want—?"

She recoiled, jumping from the sofa and nearly plastering her back against the closest wall.

Nick needed no explanation. Dark wet lashes framed eyes riveted to his shoulder holster and the service revolver tucked in it. "I'm not going to hurt you," he said quickly, softly. "I'm a cop. Nick Vincetti. A detective with the Chicago Police Department."

Those eyes that appeared more green than blue flew from his revolver back to his face. "Do you have—have proof?"

Proof? Nick nearly laughed. She had nowhere to go in the rain, and she was challenging him about identification. She'd already taken too many unnecessary chances. Driving alone in the storm, she must have veered off the main highway or she wouldn't have been so deep in the woods. "I'm going to reach back for my identification." He pinched the slim wallet from his rear pocket, flipped it open and set it on the table.

She inched closer, craning her neck to study the information. Twice she glanced from it to his face to verify that the photograph was of him. "Is this your cabin?"

With narrowed eyes, Nick studied her. What's wrong with this picture? he wondered. Again she'd gathered the blanket tighter around her shoulders and was perched on the edge of the dark green lumpy-looking sofa. Something more than fear of being with a stranger made her cower. Nick would bet his badge on that. "It belongs to a friend, my partner. Riley Garrison," he finally answered, crossing to the fireplace. As he tossed another log in the fireplace, the fire crackled. "Do you drink coffee black?"

Did she? she wondered. She nodded, not feeling steady enough to deal with the way he'd invariably look at her if she told him she didn't know.

"Why don't you tell me what you were doing out there? Did you get lost?"

Lost. Yes, she felt unbelievably lost. Avoiding his stare, she noted a couple of worn tweed chairs on the other side of the stone fireplace. Letting her gaze dance over objects, she named them. Coffeepot. Sink. Stove. You'll be all right. Don't panic. Useless as the information seemed, it meant she'd retained some knowledge. Her eyes traveled to a dented white metal cabinet with a short counter. Nearby stood a scarred oak table and chairs with arms.

Tightening fingers around the cup he'd set in front of her, she seized the comfort in its warmth. Maybe she was crazy, one of those people who lost touch with reality and wandered off aimlessly. She frowned at her hand tightly clenched around the cup. It looked unfamiliar to her, though well cared for, the nails manicured and polished. "I think I had a ring." She smoothed her thumb across her bare ring finger. "It looks like I did."

Because she kept staring at her hand, Nick angled a glance at it. Though faint, there was an indentation as though from a ring. If she expected him to search for it, she needed a wake-up call. Looking for one in the woods would be like hunting for the proverbial needle in the haystack. What he'd like is some straight answers. "Look, are you really okay?" he asked, aware of the fatigue in her eyes.

"Tired. I'm tired," she admitted.

So was he. "You can take the bed in the other room." He set the aspirin bottle and a glass of water near her. "I can't call anyone for you. There's no phone in the cabin." He thought it likely some man and possibly a family would have a few days of worry before she would be able to call home. "What's your name?" If he was giving up his bed, he would at least like to know to whom.

Lowering her head, she rubbed a hand over the top of it. If it would stop pounding, she could tell him. So what should she do? Should she lie? Pretend she remembered? Give him a phony name? Then what? No, she had to trust him. She had no other choice. Looking up, she fought for strength, but her voice broke with a rush of emotion. "I don't know."

"What do you mean, You don't know?"

"I don't know my name." There—she'd said it aloud.

"You what?" Nick took a moment to let what she'd said sink in. Dealing with people's problems came with his job, but he'd never personally had this one dropped in his lap. Maybe she wasn't telling the truth. She could be using some memory loss as an excuse because she didn't want to explain too much. "Are you saying you have amnesia?"

How simple he made that sound, she mused. Like someone might say he has a cold. This wasn't simple. Didn't he understand? She couldn't tell him anything about herself. Taking several deep breaths, she fought tears. Alone, she might cry, but not now, not yet. Using time to pull herself together, she swallowed a couple of aspirin and drank the water. Again she felt his gaze on her as if he were trying to see inside her. It's empty. You'll see nothing. She stared down at her hands and rubbed at the dry mud on the top of one of them, then at the dirt on her sweater. "Is there somewhere—" Self-consciously she touched strands of her matted hair. It felt filthy, sticky. "I'm so dirty."

It suddenly occurred to Nick how delicate she was emotionally. She sat, hugging herself as if needing to feel the presence of her own body. "I have some clothes in there." He motioned toward the duffel bag he'd hauled into the cabin earlier when he'd arrived. "Take what you need. You can change in the bedroom."

Certain that if she was clean she'd feel better, she pushed to her feet. The room spun.

In three strides, he crossed to her, catching her before she slid to the floor. "Easy."

Exhaustion weakening her, she didn't protest the arm snug around her. With each step she took, her legs felt more rubbery. And there was something so reassuring about his strong arm at her waist and the heat of his body.

Nick guided her into the bedroom, stopping beside the bed. He kept his hold on her for a moment longer. She looked far more delicate than she felt. Despite her slim appearance, the body against his was well toned. "If I let go, you're not going to pass out, are you?"

She hoped not. "No, I'm all right."

With her trembling against him, Nick didn't really believe her. "Okay." Hesitatingly he lifted his hand from her. She caught the bedpost but remained standing. "If you need anything, yell." He dropped the duffel bag she'd forgotten on the floor. "And if you're hungry, I'll cook you something when you come back out."

She nodded, nothing more. Dizziness sweeping over her, she fought it until he closed the door, then she sank to the mattress.

She'd hoped for someone to supply her with answers. Instead he'd wanted to know her name. Her name. Such a simple thing to ask a person. As she tried harder to remember, her head throbbed. For a moment, she would stay still. Only a moment. She'd spotted a mirror, felt desperate to see herself.

If only she'd known him, but even his name had meant nothing to her. She'd skimmed his address on the identification card, but what did she remember about him? Six foot one, 195 pounds. Thirty-three years old. How old was she? Forget that. Keep thinking. His birthdate. What was it? September. September 20. She'd recalled statistics about him. Only *her* past eluded her.

Why don't you know who I am? she wanted to scream. *Why don't you know me?* With her eyes half-closed, she reached back, stretching fingers for the edge of the quilt, then yanked it over her. She was cold. Too cold.

Behind her eyelids, her eyes burned with tears. She felt so alone. Empty. The hollowness within her was unbearable. How could she not remember anything personal about herself, not even the color of her eyes? What would happen to her now? What did the police do with someone who had memory loss? Would she be institutionalized? She shivered, not letting her mind imagine more, not wanting to think, and gave in to sleep.

Twice Nick checked on her to make sure she was breathing all right. The first time, he noticed that she'd never made it past the bed. Dirt had dried in her hair. Mud still smudged her delicate face. Lightly he placed a palm to her forehead and felt no heat. Moving to the foot of the bed, gently, slowly, he tugged off her boots. She never stirred. Assured her breathing was even and steady, he stepped out of the room as quietly as he'd entered.

More than once since her announcement, he'd wondered what he was going to do with her. Shifting on the lumpy sofa for the umpteenth time, he punched at one of the cushions. In the city, he would have followed procedures. He would have taken her to a hospital emergency room and forgotten about her. She would have been considered a Jane Doe and probably carted off to the county psychiatric ward or left to fend for herself. But here, in this cabin, she was his responsibility.

He slept but awoke to darkness and the storm still around him. Restless, he made a second trip into the bedroom. He made no noise, but the woman's eyes opened when he bent over her. In the dark, he watched them widen.

"What are you doing here?" she asked in a voice thick with sleep.

With a step back for her benefit, he spoke quietly. "Checking on you."

"Is it morning?"

"No. Don't talk." He'd handled witnesses who'd claimed they remembered nothing, then after questioning, pulled up some pertinent facts. He guessed the best way to treat her was like a shell-shocked witness. Question sympathetically. Go slow. "Go back to sleep," he urged, believing she needed rest the most.

Her lashes fluttered for a second, but as if craving to know something, anything to cling to before she gave in to sleep again, she spoke in a slurring manner, "Where's Rhinelander?"

"Wisconsin."

"Wisconsin?" she murmured the word. And others. "Illinois, Indiana, Michigan. What day is it?"

"November fifth."

"Then comes December. Christmas."

Deliberately Nick spoke with a softness usually reserved for more intimate moments with a woman. "Today's Sunday."

"Sunday. Monday. Tuesday." She shut her eyes and a single tear streamed down her cheek.

Bending over, Nick drew the quilt higher to her shoulders. And he wondered again, what the hell he would do with her.

Chapter Two

The gray light of dawn cast a gloominess over the room. Nick dragged on his jeans. After a night cramped on the sofa, he was ready to get up.

Yawning, he padded to the stove to plug in the coffeemaker he'd set up the night before. He remembered when he was nine years old, wandering in a fun house of mirrors at a carnival. Lost, disoriented and scared. What the woman in the next room was feeling had to be worse.

Still groggy, he tossed water from the kitchen spigot at his face. He thought about shaving and showering but rejected the idea as quickly as it formed, not wanting to wake her.

In the meantime, he began laying bacon strips into a pan. In his family, they believed food alleviated all

problems. He doubted that philosophy would work for
this woman.

The sound of rain pounding on the roof awakened
her. As she opened her eyes, the dull ache in her head
reminded her of what little she could remember. A
rainy night. Scrambling in the woods. The kindness
of a stranger.

With care, she eased from the bed and looked down
at her clothes. Had she really gone to sleep so filthy?
On steadier legs than she'd known last night, she
stood beside the bed and looked down at her stockinged feet. He'd taken off her boots. She hadn't been
aware. He could have done much more, she realized
as she crossed to the duffel bag. So she was safe.

"Take it one step at a time," she murmured while
riffling through his clothes. What shirt was his favorite? He'd said she should choose whatever she
wanted. Making any decision was overwhelming.
Swiftly she snagged a navy sweatshirt and worn-
looking jeans from the top of the bag, then inched her
way to the bathroom.

Afraid, she avoided looking in the mirror and bent
over the bathroom sink. Wetting a washcloth, she
rubbed it over her face. If only the rain would stop,
then she could leave, go to the closest town and—
and what? What would she do then?

She straightened and patted her face dry. As she
set down the towel, she realized no moment would
be easy. A stranger faced her in the mirror. Blond
hair hung straight, barely touching her shoulders. Did
she wear it like that? Was it naturally so light col-

ored? She knew she wore makeup. There were traces left behind on the towel when she'd scrubbed off the mud.

Lightly she touched the bump on her head before she stripped off dirty clothes. She was thin, too thin, she thought as she stepped into the shower. Why? Because she starved herself for a model's figure or because she exercised religiously or because of stress? Questions, so many questions.

While hot water sprayed over her, she blocked out more thoughts and frantically searched her body for scars, for any marks. Besides scratches on her hands, a few bruises dotted her knees. She doubted any of them or the one-inch scar on a kneecap could identify her.

Deliberately, to keep nerves at bay, she focused on actions—towel-drying and brushing her hair, pulling on the clothes. As she'd expected, the clothes dwarfed her. She rolled up the sleeves of the shirt and bottoms of the jeans. With a grip on the denim waistband, she ambled from the bedroom.

The smell of bacon sizzling in a pan drifted to her. So did singing. She traced her steps of the night before, then stood still, waiting at the edge of the hallway. At the stove, his back to her, he wailed out softly in a strong tenor what sounded like lyrics from an opera. His voice trailed off on a low note when he spotted her. Today would be more difficult, she knew. He'd ask questions that she'd asked of herself. Ones she had no answers for.

"Your head any clearer this morning?"

"No."

Nick poured whipped eggs into a frying pan. Not a big talker, or still scared. Regardless, he could carry conversation until she was ready. He came from a family that believed nonstop talking was a significant part of any gathering. "We're lucky. Electricity is back on."

A need to sit, more than a sense of comfort with him, made her settle on a nearby kitchen chair. She didn't feel lucky. She felt as if she were walking a precarious edge between madness and sanity.

"I'll give you something to eat, and then we'll talk."

Talk about what? she wondered, watching him fill two blue mugs with coffee. She seriously doubted food would trigger some memory. Her mind was empty. Frighteningly empty.

"Do you think you dropped your purse and jacket?"

She started to shake her head. Because movement brought a surge of a dull throbbing, she shrugged instead. A woman's whole life could be discovered in her purse. There might be photos of loved ones, makeup, credit cards—her name. And why wasn't she wearing a jacket? It was cold outside.

"If you can tell me where your car is, I'll go outside and see if I can get it running."

His voice floated around her. *A car?* Could she drive? She wasn't sure. *Everything will be fine.* She repeated those words like a mantra. "I don't know if I had a car."

"Then how did you get here?"

"I don't—" Though she started to beg off from

answering his question, she recalled too vividly the rainy trek through the woods. "I was on the ground. It was raining. I got up and began running through the woods. And—" That's when the nightmare had begun.

"And what? Did you run from the road through the woods?"

"I don't know," she muttered.

Nick gave up on questions about her past. He had a more immediate one. With the rain falling, he didn't know how long they'd be together. The idea of calling her "hey" didn't appeal to him. "Look." There was no easy way to say this, he realized. "You need to pick a name."

"A name?"

She looked away from him as if she might cry. Growing up with two sisters, Nick had witnessed his share of crying jags and expected weeping at any moment. The woman surprised him. No tears flowed. But he damned himself for rushing her. "Take your time," he said softly while placing the coffee mug on the table. "Have breakfast and—" He cut his words short as she shook her head.

Queasy, her stomach resisted the sight of the plate of eggs and bacon he was setting in front of her. "No, thank you." She saw his scowl. I'm sorry I'm a problem. He had no idea how much she wished she wasn't. "It looks good, but—"

"But you don't eat breakfast," Nick finished for her, having heard the line from other women.

"I do, but I'm not hungry today."

Nick thought that remark encouraging. Not everything was blocked out.

"Why are you here?"

"R & R," he answered. Her brow furrowed as she stared at a carton near the refrigerator containing books. "A vacation," he clarified, unsure if she'd understood. When he'd left home, he'd anticipated two weeks of solitude. The plan had changed. After the weather cleared, he would leave and take her to the city. He would help her find out who she was. Though he'd check for warrants, he assumed if she had a rap sheet, he would have remembered seeing that face.

Oh, hell, what did he know? The last time he'd believed in a woman he'd been stung. It was his own fault. He knew human nature better. Some of the sweetest-looking women in the world possessed cold, calculating minds.

Still bitter, he reflected. Five years had passed since his divorce. He enjoyed an active social life. He genuinely liked women, but he still hadn't recovered from one's pride-bruising punch.

"You like to be alone, don't you?"

"Sometimes." Taking an adjacent seat at the table, Nick salted his eggs. Worry had returned to her eyes. Fascinating eyes.

"And this is one of those times?"

He figured she had enough to handle without feeling guilty about ruining his vacation. "I don't mind company, either."

She watched him smear butter on toast. Clearly he was trying to make her feel more comfortable. She felt worse. "I thought the rain would stop by now."

She'd hoped it would. "Will the road be impass-able?"

"Probably for days if it doesn't stop raining."

Days? If she'd been standing, she knew her legs would have buckled. She would go mad waiting that long, not knowing who she was or what had happened to her.

"Did you leave your clothes in the bathroom?"

Lifting her head, she stared in puzzlement at him. Was that a trick question? Did he think she'd forgot-ten that, too? "Yes, they're—" Before she finished, in a quick move, he kicked back his chair. What did he think he would find? She'd already scrutinized them and had learned nothing. But she wasn't a po-liceman, trained to observe, gather evidence. Hanging on to a thread of hope, she bolted and followed. She reached the bathroom door to see him fingering the heavy white sweater and the jeans. "What can you tell from them?"

They'd cost more than he made in a month, Nick calculated. Both had designer labels. The boots were Italian leather. "Unless you stole these, I'd say you're rich or deeply in debt."

"So this is nothing but guesswork."

Nick had tried to put himself in her shoes, show understanding, but he thought he'd offered encour-agement. "Right. This is called guesswork," he said irritably to her back as she whipped away. Bent on making his point, he followed her. "Whether you re-alize it or not," he said, when joining her at the table, "we have a key to your background. You're probably related to or know some influential people. Someone

will most likely be looking for you.'' She looked fragile, almost breakable suddenly. ''I don't know anything for sure,'' he said, between bites of cold eggs.
''But if I'm right, then you're not homeless, you're
not someone with no family or background who fends
for herself. You have people who care. That would
be in your favor. That would mean this is all temporary. So for now, let's find out what you do know.''

''I told you—''

Her hint of temper didn't faze him. Nick thought
she had every right to be angry. And in his family,
people yelled with the same quickness that they
laughed. ''I know. Nothing,'' he finished for her
while taking his plate to the sink. Through his experience, he'd learned that some answers didn't come
easily or quickly. ''By the time we get out of here,
you might have remembered everything.''

What if she didn't? she wondered. Fear floated over
her like a heavy cloud. He could make such a statement. He wasn't the one going through this. He
wasn't the one who'd lost all connection to a life.

While water rushed over the plate, Nick rolled a
shoulder that felt tight from a restless night on the
sofa. ''If you don't try to remember, we won't
know.''

Suddenly cold, she sipped more of the steaming
coffee but couldn't touch the toast. She shouldn't be
so unreasonable. He'd offered her shelter, clothing,
food. He'd been trying to help. But she'd wanted him
to tell her who she was. She'd wanted a miracle from
him.

''Here. You look as if you need something for

that,'' he said, motioning to her hand clutching the denim. She reached forward for the rope, doing her best to appear calm, but he noticed her hands trembled when she threaded the rope through the loops of the jeans. ''It doesn't make any sense to me that you were this far in the woods. There's no reason to leave the paved highway unless you were coming to one of these cabins. Think you were meeting someone?''

Someone? She angled a look at him. Did he mean a man? ''I don't know.''

Nick turned away, frowning. Was the highway flooded further north? That would explain why she'd go off it. She might have been looking for shelter to stop and made the turn onto the dirt road. People didn't always act sensibly when faced with difficult situations. They walked in the desert, stripping off clothes, leaving themselves unprotected. They left damp clothes on when stuck in blizzards, encouraging frostbite. ''If you think you can tell me what direction you came from, I'll go out and look around for a purse or a car.''

Not looking up, she shrugged.

Nick said nothing. He'd expected depression. Who wouldn't feel like hell in her situation? Leaving the room, he wandered into the bathroom. Without thought, he picked up her dirty clothes piled in a corner, plunged her jeans into a sink full of water, then scrubbed the mud off them. Playing nursemaid now, Vincetti. Wouldn't the guys at the precinct love that idea?

Well, so what? He wrung out the jeans and the sweater, then flung them over the shower rod. Washing a few clothes bothered him less than not being able to help her, not finding the truth. He hated failing at anything.

The biggest failure in his life had been his marriage. There had been a time in the beginning of it when the days had carried the promise of forever. He'd thought those were the best of days. He'd liked having a woman around, smelling her familiar sweetness first thing in the morning, sharing soft talk after a night of loving. He'd liked the intimacy of knowing another person's movements, understanding her moods. Or so he'd thought.

In the beginning, he'd been flattered by Julia's attention. In the end, he'd understood that she'd been playing out a whim, but he'd never understood her.

Softly he cursed, annoyed with himself, and snatched up his parka hanging on a hallway doorknob. Rehashing history made no sense. The marriage had ended; he had no regrets now. "I'm going outside," he said, returning to the other room and pausing long enough to slip on gloves.

Spiky dark lashes shadowing her face lifted quickly to pin him with a wide-eyed stare. She looked as scared now as she'd been earlier.

"I could go with."

Immediately Nick nixed the idea of her traipsing around behind him, especially in those heeled boots. "I won't be long," he assured her while zipping his parka.

Any amount of time would be too long to suit her. "Detective—"

Deep-set, dark eyes came back to her. "Nick," he corrected.

"I want to thank you."

"I haven't done anything."

Quietly he closed the door behind him. She really didn't want to be alone. Setting her palms on the table, she stared hard at them. Her hands no longer looked so strange to her. Well-manicured nails, expensive clothes. Was she a wealthy woman or one who lived beyond her means? Was she loving or unemotional?

She tried to pass time reading one of the books he'd brought. She couldn't concentrate. Time ticked by with unbelievable slowness. How long had he been gone? Several hours? What if he didn't come back? He would. Relax.

Head back, she shut her eyes. As a child, had she liked dolls? Had she skipped rope? Had she lived in a house or climbed steps to an apartment? Had she...?

More thoughts were forgotten as a ringing filled her ears, as a bright light suddenly pierced behind her eyes. Someone was running down a curving staircase. Running down endless steps. Running toward what?

She snapped open her eyes. Was that her? The image had come and gone too quickly. What if that's all she ever saw?

Bounding from the chair, she smothered an urge to cry and paced to the window, then away and back again. For a few seconds, she wanted some escape from the dull throbbing in her head, from the unanswered questions. She couldn't stay here, alone, with only her thoughts. If she looked around outside, she might find something.

She fished a pair of Nick's socks from the duffel bag, then wiggled her feet into her heeled boots. With luck, she wouldn't break her neck, but she wasn't feeling too lucky.

Outside rain pounded harder. She still had a problem. No jacket and no rainwear. Again she rummaged through his duffel bag. Needing to make one stop before she left the cabin, she strolled to the bathroom while cuffing up the sleeves of his jogging jacket.

Tears smarted her eyes as she saw her washed clothes. How much kindness would a stranger give? He'd already offered so much. Temptation nudged her to take the easy way, to lean on him. She resisted the idea instantly. She needed to solve her own problem. *How* was the big question.

Angrily she yanked down the shower curtain to use as a raincoat and wrapped it around her. She believed she had two choices. She could wallow in her despair and pray someone was looking for her. Or she could fight to retrieve memories.

Cuddling deeper in the oversize jogging jacket, she opened the cabin door. As cold rain flew at her face, she barreled forward. She'd already made a decision. She wasn't going to sit around and do nothing.

Head bent, Nick tramped through mud from the dirt road and the bridge. Clumps of mud coated the bottom of his boots, and he stopped by a rock to scrape the mire from them. He'd spent the past few moments considering how much to tell her. He knew zilch about how to deal with someone who had amnesia. All he could do was follow instincts. If he were in her place, he would want people to be truthful and...

The sound of sticks breaking beneath footsteps whipped him around. Blinking hard against the rain, he thought he was falling prey to imagination. What looked like a shower curtain moved amidst brush. Then he saw the strands of pale hair poking out from the hood of a jacket, *his* jogging jacket.

Rain dripping off her, she labored up the muddy incline and stomped to the top. Instead of self-pity, what he interpreted as resolve darkened her eyes. "What did you learn?"

Plenty, Nick mused. She did exactly what she wanted to do. "Come on. Let's go back to the cabin."

"You didn't answer my question. What did you find?"

He swung a look at her, at the hand on his arm. "There's a section of broken railing at the bridge, but I doubt a car went through it."

"What do we do now?" She kept her grip on him as if determined to get answers.

Nick had too much experience not to recognize the quick stirring in his blood. Though he didn't expect the reaction, he understood it. Besides beauty, she'd revealed what an elderly uncle of his referred to as moxie. She also had eyes that promised to haunt a man if he wasn't careful. "When we're out of here, I'll call authorities. They'll look."

Rubbing numbed hands together, she frowned at his back for a second, then copied his steps down a nearby path. A bridge? She'd nodded, not wanting to

tell him that she didn't remember one. When she'd
touched him, she'd immediately wished she hadn't.
Intense-looking eyes had fixed on her. Butterflies had
fluttered in her stomach, but she'd willed herself to
stand firm, to get answers. He'd been outside too long
for her to believe he'd learned nothing.

Cold and soaked, she plodded up the cabin steps
as he detoured toward the Jeep. Aware of the mud
clinging to her boots, she paused on the porch to yank
off her right boot and nearly lost her balance. Falling
on her backside would cinch this day. In stockinged
feet, she carried her boots into the warm cabin and
set them on a doormat.

For a few moments, she stood near the fire, letting
its heat radiate through her. Still cold, she eyed the
thick coffee in the bottom of the pot, then began rummaging through the bottom cupboards. She knew
there was milk, orange juice, even beer. What she
wanted was a cup of hot tea.

To search the bottom cupboards, she dropped to her
knees and bent forward. She was groping in the back
of the white cabinet, when behind her, she heard the
door open. Over her shoulder, she saw him with his
boots in hand.

"What are you looking for?"

"A tea bag."

"Tea?" His lips curved into more of an amused
smirk than a smile.

"I guess not," she muttered, and resigned herself
to another cup of coffee.

Nick plunked a frying pan onto the stove. Whether
she liked it or not, he had to make her face facts. "No

one can help you remember, except you.'' Palming an onion, he lounged against the refrigerator. ''You know that, don't you?''

''I'm trying to remember.''

In fascination, Nick watched light dance across her hair with her movement.

''I wonder about everything, not just myself. I know so much, and nothing. I can name colors, read and comprehend, recall historical facts, but my past still remains a mystery. I don't even know what I like to do. That's important. It would tell me what kind of a person I am, wouldn't it?''

Nick nearly smiled. When she got going, she did it at full speed.

''When you were in the woods, did you see a car?'' she asked.

''No.'' He turned the pork chops, which were now sizzling in the pan. ''But that doesn't mean there wasn't one.''

That made sense. Just because he hadn't found one didn't mean it was nonexistent. Snatching up the book she'd been reading earlier, she plopped onto the closest chair. A car was somewhere. How else could she have gotten here? She concentrated hard, trying to visualize it. Like before, her mind remained blank except for more questions. Why was she in the isolated woods? If she'd been driving, could she have gone off the road and into the water and not remembered? No answers again. Sighing, she closed the book and inhaled the aroma of onions mixed into fried potatoes. ''That smells wonderful.''

Nick nodded a thanks. He gave her an A for effort.

Some women in her situation would have curled up in a corner and wept buckets.

"I've been thinking about what you said."

Scooping up a hearty serving of the potatoes, he delivered them and a pork chop to a plate and handed it to her. "About what?"

"A name." She sampled a potato before she sat at the table. "I'd like you—" She paused as lights flickered. "I'd like you to call me Ann."

Nick masked his surprise at her choice. She'd chosen a simple name, a common one. He recalled his ex-wife had had a friend named Annelise who'd used that nickname. She'd also used petty cash that equated to a few thousand dollars. "Does it mean something to you?"

"No. I didn't even think about it," she said between bites. "Do you like it?"

"I like it," he answered, joining her at the table. He couldn't quite pigeonhole her and that bothered him. He was trained to observe, analyze, make snap judgments.

As thunder rumbled threateningly above the roof, Ann jumped. Through the window, she saw fingers of lightning stabbing downward. Another roar of thunder followed. She obviously didn't like storms. As a child, had she buried herself beneath covers when lightning brightened the dark sky? "I really do wish it would stop raining." She struggled against her own skittishness. The weather didn't help. Lights flickered again, and with another clap of thunder, blackness surrounded her. She scrambled to a stand, feeling even more alone suddenly. "Nick? Where are you?"

"Just a minute." He heard a trace of panic in her voice and inched closer. Dammit, where was his duffel bag and the flashlight?

Cautiously Ann took several steps. Again thunder crashed with nerve-grating harshness. "Where are you?"

"I'm near the sofa."

Following the sound of his voice, she about-faced and collided with him. Beneath her palm at his chest, she felt his heart beating strong and steady. Hers beat harder. You're not alone. Not alone, she repeated to herself.

The room lit with an eerie flash. She gripped his upper arm tighter. Strength. She felt it, tried to absorb it. "I—" Whatever she planned to say lodged in her throat. She stared into his eyes, watching them roam slowly down her face to her mouth, and couldn't nudge herself from the hard, sturdy body against hers. Something warm and slow moved inside her. With a start, she jerked away. Only then did she notice the electricity was on. Taking a long breath, her heart still pounding, she ordered herself to relax. Was that possible? She slanted a look at him. Don't overreact. Nothing happened, not really. She'd been scared; he'd grabbed her. Her emotions were close to the surface. She might have felt much more than he had. Sitting again, she dug into dinner and kept quiet until she was sure she'd sound calm. "Did you listen to the radio in the Jeep?"

He'd heard the news. "Yes." Nick said the words

without a glance her way. While a storm raged outside, a slow-building one was brewing within him.
During those moments of darkness, he'd only had to
lower his head, bring his mouth an inch closer, then...
Nothing, he told himself. She had enough problems
without him adding to them. He had to think about
her as a case he'd been assigned to. Forget flawless
skin that invited a man's caress. Forget that smile.
Sinking back in his chair, he damned the rain. The
constant hammering was getting on his nerves.

"Did you hear anything about a missing woman?"

Nick stalled, scooping potatoes on his fork. He had
to tell her, didn't he? Looking up, he met a gaze filled
with questions. "No, I didn't."

"Nothing?"

He didn't need to be a mind reader to guess her
thoughts. Why wasn't someone missing her? Was
there no one who cared about her?

In an impatient movement, she pushed off the
chair. "I hate this." Despite the anger in her voice,
she looked ready to cry. "I really hate this."

Nick believed her. Repeatedly he'd seen her re-
sisting tears, demanding a toughness from herself that
she appeared too delicate to possess. Standing by the
window, she looked so needy, not for him or any
man, but for closeness with someone. There was little
he could say or do.

Lightly he touched her shoulders and turned her to
gather her in his arms. "The answers are near. We
just haven't found them yet." How many times had
he courted the same thought during an investigation?
Others had described him as relentless, dogged. A fair

share of criminals had cursed him because of such traits. Those might be the ones she needed most. He drew her closer, stroking her hair. As she sagged against him, he felt her draw calming breaths. He felt womanly softness. And he held her longer than he should have.

Chapter Three

Before dawn, Nick was outside chopping wood. He wasn't sleeping well. He would have liked to blame that on the lumpy sofa. He would have liked to, but knew better. One classy-looking blonde was bothering him a lot. With a last split of a log, he bent over and gathered the wood. Arms full, he shoved the door open with his shoulder.

At the stove, Ann only glanced his way. "I'm beginning to hate rain."

She echoed Nick's thoughts. When he'd awakened, he'd groaned as he'd heard the rain pelting the cabin's roof.

"I almost wish it would snow."

"That's just what we need," he said while peeling off his wet parka.

Pouring milk into a shallow dish, Ann sloughed

away the tinge of sarcasm in his voice. Perhaps it was his comforting hug last night that made her feel less tense around him. She assumed that made sense. He was her only link to a world beyond a rainy night in the woods. Considering her problem, it seemed logical that this man, the only person she knew in the world, wouldn't seem like a stranger anymore. But when she left here, everyone else would. What if there was a special man in her life? What if she felt nothing for him anymore? The thought was too sad to consider. She yearned to know someone loved her. If—when she found that person, she wanted to love back.

"What are you making?"

"French toast." She gave him a slim smile, then shoved the spatula under a slice of bread and flipped it. Sort of brown. But not golden brown. What was she doing wrong? She plopped the slice of French toast on a plate. "It's good you can cook, because I don't think I can. Which seems odd. After all, everyone knows how to cook, don't they?"

Nick had dated a few women who'd barely managed to heat soup. "Do they?" he asked offhandedly while he eyed the soggy-looking toast on his plate. Her version of French toast wouldn't win any culinary awards.

"Why do you do that?" she asked without any real irritation.

Using conversation to stall the eating, he dropped to a chair. "Do what?"

"You answer with questions."

An urge to grin jabbed at him. "Training. 'Am I

under arrest?' they usually ask.'' He poked his fork into his breakfast. '''Should you be?' I answer.''

''And they feel intimidated?''

Nick arched a brow. ''Hopefully.''

She gave him a semblance of a smile. ''What makes a man learn to cook so well?''

Nick shifted on the chair as she settled again to drink her coffee. ''I could give you some story about trying to impress women, but the truth is that my parents own a restaurant. Everyone in my family cooks,'' he answered between chews. Somehow he'd endured several bites of the wet French toast. If she'd cooked it longer, it might have been good.

Ann cradled her coffee cup and regarded him over the rim of it. If only he was less—less what? Thoughtful? Handsome? Everything? ''You're from a big family?''

''The list is too long.'' Nick patted himself on the back for braving his way through a whole slice of toast. ''Why aren't you eating?''

''I wasn't really hungry. But I wanted to see if I could cook.'' She'd decided she was lousy at it, and he deserved some award for not wanting to hurt her feelings. Nick set down his fork and took a hearty swallow of coffee. ''Thanks for breakfast,'' he said, rising to leave the room.

Alone, Ann sighed. Whenever he left her by herself, she felt as if the walls of the cabin were closing in on her. There was no peace with only the company of her own thoughts.

She wandered to the cabin door and opened it. The sound of rain drummed against the ground, and dismal gray clouds hung like a thick blanket of dirty cotton over the woods.

Placing a hand on the doorknob, she began to shut the door and stilled as she thought she saw movement in the bushes. Eyes narrowing, she scrutinized a clump of brush. Did they have bears here? "Nick!" she yelled once, then again as she dashed for his shoulder holster and gun on a nearby chair.

Before she raced back to the door, he charged into the room, hitting the kitchen floor on a skid. "What's the matter?"

Her back to him, Ann didn't give him more than a glance. "Something is out there," she said from the doorway.

What was out there meant diddly to Nick. His gaze shot to his shoulder holster dangling from her hand. In two strides, he crossed to her and grabbed it. "Give me that. What did you see?" he asked, shouldering forward to shield her with his body.

"I didn't exactly see anything. I heard something." Ann peered over his shoulder, setting a hand on his back. She knew a woman couldn't be too careful. In the city, women were always on alert, needing to be cautious. *City.* That was a memory. She was from the city. But which city?

Instead of a bear, a man suddenly popped out from behind shrubs. Nick judged him to be in his early fifties. Wearing a ranger's jacket and worn Levi's, he bowed his head against a gust of wind as he reached the clearing for the cabin.

Reaching back, Nick placed the holster on the floor by the door, then started forward to meet him.

Ann snagged his arm. "What are you doing?"

If the grip on his arm hadn't stopped him, the alarm in her voice would have. "I'm going to talk to him."

"How do you know he's a ranger? He could be anyone."

By anyone, Nick assumed that she meant some psychopath.

"Hi, folks," the man called out, nearly to the cabin stairs now. "I'm from the lookout tower. Horace Kemp."

"Lookout tower," Nick repeated to her before stepping out the door. While the ranger climbed the steps, Nick waited on the porch and used the towel he'd brought with him from the bathroom to wipe shaving cream from his jaw. "Nick Vincetti," he said, offering his hand.

Red cheeked from the cold, the man gazed curiously over Nick's shoulder at Ann standing in the doorway. "Kind of late in the season to be up here."

The solitude had lured Nick. He'd wanted time to relax, to forget photographs of victims. "I needed to get away from the job for a few weeks," he said simply, aware Ann had moved close behind him. Whether or not she believed the man was who he appeared to be, she'd obviously let curiosity lead her. "We've been stuck here because of the storm. Are the roads okay?"

"For safety's sake, wait until this rain stops unless you have to leave right away."

Nick shivered, wishing he'd grabbed his jacket. "Want some coffee?"

"No, I have to be going. There are a few more

places to check, though I think they're closed for the winter. You'd better go in before you freeze.''

"Wait one minute.'' His fingertips numbing from the cold, Nick tucked them into the short pockets of his Levi's. "There's something I want to talk to you about.'' As concisely as possible, he told the ranger his credentials, then filled him in on Ann's dilemma.

"She doesn't know who she is.'' He riveted a questioning stare on Nick. "Do you have identification?'' he asked, frowning now.

During the past few minutes, Ann had shifted uncomfortably. Being talked about as if she were invisible was nearly as bad as not knowing who she was. "I'll get it,'' she offered tightly, unable to keep irritation out of her voice.

Nick detected the hint of temper in her voice. "My wallet is on the table.'' Without another word, she spun around with her head up and shoulders back. Proud. Maybe too proud, too independent, he mused, aware of how often she'd battled herself before leaning on him. "How far away is the sheriff's office?'' he asked, giving the ranger his attention again.

"About forty miles east of here. Why do you ask?''

"I need local authorities to search for a car off the road. A license plate number could reveal her identity.''

"I have a CB at the ranger station. I could do that for you,'' he said in a more cooperative tone. "Does she need to go to a hospital?''

"No, physically she's doing all right. When we leave here, I'll take her to one in Chicago.''

"Is that where she wants to go?'' he asked, more

to Ann than him as she joined them, clutching Nick's worn-looking, black leather wallet.

While the ranger read his identification, Nick slipped into the jacket she'd brought with her. "Thanks." He felt nerves in the hand that brushed his. "I told him that we'll go to Chicago."

"Think you're from there?" the ranger asked and handed Nick's wallet back to him.

She mustered up what Nick viewed as her best smile. "I don't know."

"Heck of a thing." The ranger shook his head and offered her a few sympathetic words. "Don't worry. I'll call the sheriff's office for you."

A gust whirling around him, Nick gazed up at the dark heavy clouds. "Do you think we'll get snow before morning?"

The ranger snorted. "Can happen anytime. Sure you don't need anything?" he asked Ann, almost with fatherly concern.

"No, I'm fine." Of course, she wasn't. Her life was out of control. She shivered in the bitter cold air and left them to reenter the cabin. While Nick stayed outside, talking to the ranger, edgy, she sought anything to keep busy.

The rest of the morning she dusted, read several chapters of a book and devoured half a dozen cookies. Spotting a newspaper Nick had brought with him, she spread it out on the table. No one could help her but herself. Had she always believed that? By nature, was she independent? Would everything come back to her? What if it didn't? How could a person not even know what they were like, what pleased them, what made them tick? Don't panic, she chided herself, feeling that emotion rising. She took a stabilizing breath to quell the pressure swelling in her chest. Were seesawing emotions a symptom of amnesia? Was that why one minute she felt almost cheerful and the next weepy?

With the squeak of the door opening, chilly air sliced through the room. Except for sharing a few quiet moments with her, Nick had made himself scarce. She reminded herself that he'd chosen such isolation in the woods while she was craving to escape the one of her mind's making. "Is it colder outside?"

"Yeah. That's old news, you know," he said as she remained bent over the newspaper.

More than anything, Ann longed for conversation. "Not to me."

"Learn anything?"

His dark hair glistening from the damp air, he stood still in front of the warmth of the fireplace. Was it his ability to stand so still, to be so quiet, that made him a good cop? "Some names and places sounded familiar."

"Like what?" With interest, Nick turned toward her, noticing she'd washed and dried the dishes. He'd believed he'd made an accurate guess about her background. Now he had to reconsider his first impression of her. He'd met his share of Julia's wealthy friends. Not one of them would have ruined her manicure with menial tasks.

Ann closed the newspaper and folded it. "Two warring countries have decided on a truce, a rock star

married, and an early and unexpected snowfall para-
lyzed Pittsburgh.'' To her surprise, when she'd read
the stock exchange, she'd understood it. ''And I knew
that Steel Evans is the lead singer for Cruddy Blues.''

That stirred his smile. He'd never heard of Cruddy
Blues. ''So you are remembering?''

''It seems so.'' Munching on a cookie, Ann stared
out at the woods. ''I wonder what I do,'' she said,
more to herself than Nick.

Nick paused in opening a book and looked up, this
time to see her bending over the carton of books.
Strands of hair fell across her cheek. As he dodged a
thought of burying his hand in the softness, he swore
at the idiocy that was threatening to settle in. He
needed to think of her objectively. No other way. He
would help her find out where she belonged. He
would protect her. What he would stop doing was
looking at her all the time like some kid who'd just
discovered females.

''So what do you think?'' With a book in her hand,
a medical thriller, she twisted and bent at the waist.

''What do I think about what?'' he asked, having
to concentrate on what she was saying.

''What kind of work I do.''

From what he'd detected so far, he thought her
question odd. ''Why do you think you do anything?''

She kept on moving, stretching first to one side and
then the other. ''Everyone does.''

He had an ex-wife who'd never worked a day in
her life. ''What are you doing?''

Her hair swung as she straightened. ''Exercising.''

Nick nearly groaned when once more she gave him

a tantalizing view of her backside. She moved with an agile grace, reminding him of an aerobics instructor he'd dated for several months. "Do you think you should be doing that? You were clobbered the other night."

Ann stilled and frowned at him. "Do you believe someone hit me?"

Nick gave up trying to read. Hell-bent on talking, she'd allowed him few minutes of silence. "It was an expression."

"Oh, I feel fine. No dizziness anymore. And I think—I think I must work out because this feels—I don't know—good."

Having touched her a few times, he'd have made a similar guess. She was lean and well toned. She was also soft in the perfect places.

Ann stilled, watching him set the book on a table. "I thought that was a good story. Didn't you like it?"

Nick switched mental gears. "You remember reading it?"

"I saw the movie." As his eyes flicked to her with a questioning alertness, Ann rushed words. "Before you ask, I'll tell you that I don't know when I saw it or if I saw it with someone." She'd been excited when she'd touched the book and had remembered the movie. She'd even recalled the actors' names. But nothing else. Would hypnosis help her to remember more about herself? But how would she afford that? She had no money, no job. She was in limbo. When they left the cabin, she had no idea where she would go.

"Ann?"

It took a moment for her to acknowledge that he was talking to her. "I forgot my name," she murmured in what sounded like a self-deprecating tone.

Nick responded to her slim smile, one, he assumed because of the sadness clouding her eyes, that she'd worked hard for.

"I meant the name I made up. I wonder why I can't remember my own."

She sent him one of those quick, uncertain smiles. He felt his gut tighten disturbingly. "Ann is a nice name."

"But is it mine? And how old am I?" She sighed softly and meandered to the window. Leaves fluttered beneath the wind. Though still daytime, a darkness fell on the woods. With a turn from the window, she unconsciously hunted in the food carton, then dipped her hand into the box of cookies again. "I wonder if I like to be alone or have a lot of friends."

What sounded like a plea for an answer came out on a whisper. All Nick could offer was a token of reassuring words. "You like to talk a lot. I don't think you're a loner."

"Are you subtly trying to tell me something?"

His lips tugged up at one corner at what he considered her stab at humor. "No one has ever described me as subtle."

Perhaps not, but what about kind, caring? Ann wondered. The mix of gentle and strong in him would appeal to a lot of women. Only the other day, she'd felt so unlucky, and she knew now she'd been blessed in finding someone whose kindness and understanding had lessened the impact of some difficult moments for her. She considered, too, that she could have been stuck with some grisly mountain man who believed a daily shower would rust his bones. She had been lucky. The man with her was likable and handsome. Back to that again. But he was really handsome, she decided.

"Got another problem?" Nick asked, because of her frown.

Hundreds, it seemed, including an undeniable attraction for him. "Beyond the obvious?" she asked, unable to veil her frustration. More than once she'd wondered, why her? Why had this happened to her? "Any other observations?"

Some he had no business having, Nick reflected. "Only more guesswork."

Ann slanted a look at him. Was that a curt reminder of her own words the other day? "I was being snotty when I said that to you."

"I hope you're not waiting for me to disagree."

The amusement in his eyes nudged another smile from her. "Do you want an apology?"

"For what? Saying what was on your mind?"

He would be honest even if it was painful. Ann viewed that trait as important. Why was it? If only she understood herself better, knew the reason for some emotions. "I value your guesswork," she said truthfully.

That comment brought his head up. "My observations could be about as accurate as what you'd learn from a palm reader," Nick answered, though the pleasure from her compliment was lingering in him.

"You're a bit of a cynic, aren't you?"

"About whatever I can't explain."

Ann would have expected that. More than once, he'd conveyed a no-nonsense attitude. "I'll take my chances. Tell me what else you think about me."

Nick caught a tinge of desperation in her voice. "I think you're educated."

Questioningly Ann inclined her head, waiting for him to explain.

"You filled in some empty blanks in the crossword puzzle that had me stymied. Foreign phrases, scientific names," he added as an explanation.

Was she bilingual? Maybe a scientist? More guesswork, she thought disgustedly. "I *know* something I bet you haven't noticed. I love these cookies," she said, reaching for another one.

Leaning back in his chair, Nick folded his hands behind his head. "Or have an insatiable sweet tooth."

"I have eaten half the box, haven't I? And they're probably your favorites," she said, between bites.

"Actually, they aren't." Nick crossed to the refrigerator. "They're my mother's. She knew I was taking this trip and shoved a box at me before I could get in my car."

She couldn't imagine too many people intimidating or persuading him to do what he didn't want to. "She has wonderful taste."

Nick smiled back at her. Keep moments friendly. Just friendly, he reminded himself. He had enough to think about without complicating everything. Opening the refrigerator door, he surveyed the food that was left. He'd packed for one, not two. They'd be all right until the end of the week. After that, if the rain continued, he'd have to ration food. That seemed unlikely to him. The rain would probably stop before nightfall.

It didn't. It drenched the already-soaked ground. Standing by the window after dinner, Nick peered past the bare, tangled limbs of the tree that shaded the cabin from a summer sun. The wind howled. Lightning flashed, revealing puddles but no layer of water. Still the trip out wouldn't be easy.

As for the woman behind him, sitting near the fireplace, repeatedly, almost effortlessly, she kept clicking something on inside him. There was something too easy about sitting and spending companionable time with her. The moments held a domestic edge, an intimacy that he'd looked for in his marriage and had never found. Shifting his stance, he watched her stretch her legs out in front of the fire.

"It's odd the things that come to me." Bracing a hand behind her, she crossed her legs at the ankles and wiggled stockinged toes as if warming them.

"Like what?" She looked relaxed. He wasn't. Light slanted across her face, casting the edge of her lips and the curve of her jaw in shadow, tempting his touch.

"The first morning I was here, I heard you singing and knew it was an opera, but I couldn't recall the name of it. I remember now. *La Traviata.* Do you always sing when you cook?"

"Habit."

Ann sat forward to wrap her arms around her bent

knees, her attention shifting to him at the kitchen sink. A masculine man with strong hands, he showed no self-consciousness in cooking or washing dishes.

"When I was a kid, my mother had a phonograph player in a walk-in pantry. Every day I'd come home after school to great smells and the sound of music. She wore out Caruso records." A grin split his face. "Is it your turn to analyze?"

She wished she could, but he wasn't an easy man to understand. He would smile, talk freely, seem to offer friendship. But often enough, before she could draw her next breath, she noticed the grim set of his mouth. "You're not an open book."

"Neither are you," he assured her.

"That's true." Ann watched him stack plates. Plain white plates. "I don't even know me..." Unconsciously she let the last word trail off. Flowers belonged on plates. Delicate, miniature flowers. And gold trim at the plate's rim.

Nick paused in reaching for the silverware in the drain rack. Something in the tilt of her head alerted him. As a frown settled and deepened on her face, he stepped within her vision, but she kept staring through him as if tranced. Uncertain, he caught her arm, touching it as impersonally as possible.

"I saw a plate. Isn't that silly?" Bewilderment edged her voice. "Plates and staircases and—"

Nick squatted beside her. "What staircase?"

"I had a dream about a staircase. Well, it wasn't a dream. A memory, I guess."

"What did you see?"

"Nothing much," she said quickly. In fact, she'd

even forgotten about it because none of that had seemed significant. "I saw a curving staircase." Her brows knit. "And heard what sounded like a ringing telephone."

Nick had hoped for more. He saw no importance in staircases and chinaware.

She could tell he wasn't impressed. Neither am I, she wanted to say. Standing, she eyed the playing cards on a badly scratched end table. "What were you playing?"

Nick followed the movement of her arm. "Solitaire."

"Do you play gin rummy?"

"Do you?"

She hadn't given it much thought. Puzzled, she frowned with her answer. "I guess I do."

Maybe he'd slotted her wrong. Julia had gone to weekly bridge club meetings and sipped Perrier at polo matches. Where he'd come from, people played gin rummy and poker and ate hot dogs at baseball games. "Do you remember who you played with?" he asked, looking beyond the obvious.

In answer, she shook her head, then ambled to the table, grabbing the deck of cards. "So do you want to play?"

It wasn't difficult to guess that she was looking for distractions from the questions in her mind. "Sure."

"Penny a point?"

That sounded like a hustle to him, so he wasn't surprised that she played with experience. She was also lucky, he soon learned. And slick. She handled the cards better than some Las Vegas dealers. Not for the first time since they'd started playing, she set down her cards and announced gin.

During the next hour, Nick's admiration for her grew. If he'd unexpectedly walked in on the scene, he'd never have guessed the chaos within her.

While he dealt the cards, Ann gazed out the window. The coldness seemed to seep inside though no chill drifted into the cabin. Christmas would be soon. Would she know who she was by then?

"Tired of playing?" Nick questioned. As she shook her head, he wished he could read her better. Was she worrying? He couldn't stop himself from asking a question, one that women usually asked him, one he found annoying. "What are you thinking about?"

"Holidays. I wonder if I like them. If I've had happy ones."

"They're not always perfect." Nick thought of one that had played out disastrously but usually brought family laughter with the recall. He gave what she seemed to want most—something other than herself to think about. "We spent one Christmas without a tree because my aunt's cat kept jumping in it. Never liked that cat."

"You're smiling."

She was, too. He liked seeing her this way, liked the dimple in her cheek, liked the way the light from the fire danced across her hair.

Ann couldn't help wondering if she had a past like him, possibly one filled with similar warm and humorous or tender moments. "It was a happy time, wasn't it?'' Her attention drifted back to the cards, especially the three jacks he'd played.

"You're right. It was, but no one would have thought so at the time.'' His voice trailed off as she laid down three kings, a run of hearts and played her jack on the ones he'd set down.

"Gin,'' she announced.

With feigned disgust, Nick tossed the rest of his cards on the table. "Enough.'' He had no problem losing at cards. What bothered him more was the temptation coursing through him to touch that hair, to feel its silkiness again.

Ann would have liked to thank him, but thought he might not understand how grateful she was. For a while, a sense of normalcy had slipped over her. But he deserved a thank-you for another reason. "Nick, about last night.'' She crossed to the sink and leaned back against the counter. "Thank you. I needed someone to hold me.''

Not certain how to respond, he shrugged a shoulder.

"I know you felt sorry for me.''

If he'd been smart, he would have let her believe that's all he'd felt, but he wasn't always smart. "Don't pin any merit badges on me.'' He didn't deserve any. He'd had more than a few thoughts that weren't so honorable.

Ann thought he was trying to make her smile, then she watched his eyes move over her face to her lips. This time she wasn't imagining the sensation of warmth flowing through her. With a look, he caressed her though he wasn't touching her. Did other men do that to her? When they looked at her, did she feel this way? When they did, what did they see? "Do you find me pretty?" The moment the words slipped out, Ann wanted to snatch them back.

Nick wondered how she could look in a mirror and still feel the need to ask that question. "You want compliments?"

She supposed she had. But mostly she'd wanted honesty. She'd wanted to know how a man viewed her—how *he* did. Now she felt like an idiot for asking. She turned to avoid his eyes. "Forget it," she insisted, waving a hand as if to ward off more discussion.

He wouldn't let her.

Before she could move a few steps, Nick blocked her path. "I don't think you're pretty." Against his better judgment, he closed the few inches between them. The need to touch her intensified. "Beautiful." As he traced his thumb across her cheekbone, his fingers itched to feel more of her skin. "I'd say you're beautiful," he said softly.

Ann didn't move, couldn't, as he kept her close with one hand at her waist while his other framed her face. Her heart quickened, beating faster when he lowered his face by inches until it was a hairbreadth from hers. She wanted his kiss. She expected it, the full pressure of his mouth against hers. Instead, his lips brushed hers as if testing.

In her eyes, Nick read questions. He could have told her that he wanted more than a sampling of her taste. But he was a pragmatic man, one who believed actions carried consequences. Even with an ache gnawing at him, he chose the smartest course of action. He stepped back. "I have to get more wood." He reached back and snatched up his jacket. What he wanted didn't matter.

Chapter Four

Before going to bed, Ann convinced herself that she needed a friend more than a lover. She realized she had a problem when she awakened the next morning with Nick on her mind. He ignited something dangerously close to desire within her. And at this time in her life, she definitely didn't have any room for that.

Ambling from the bedroom, she found him packing cans into a carton. A glance at the window was all the explanation she needed. "It stopped raining."

"Before dawn."

"We're leaving?" With his nod, Ann moved beside him. "What can I do?"

A loaded question, Nick thought. He'd spent a long night thinking about her. Because he believed in honesty, even when it made him uncomfortable, he faced the truth squarely. In less than a few days, she'd pulled at him with her apprehension and with her courage. She appealed to him as much as she puzzled him. He had to admit that she did a lot that he never anticipated, like trudging in the rain through the woods while wearing a shower curtain and grabbing his service revolver to defend herself. He assumed that might be why she kept tripping responses within him. He'd always been a sucker for strength during adversity. She'd already proved she possessed a fair share of it. "I left cereal on the table," he said when she finally stepped away.

That he'd acted as if the moments the night before hadn't existed made sense to Ann. He'd paid her a compliment, one she'd practically begged to get. So she knew now that he found her attractive. So sensation had skittered up her spine. So a slow-moving heat had swept through her. She needed to keep a clear head.

By nine, Nick had carted the last carton into the Jeep. Entering the cabin, he unzipped his parka, then held it for her to slip into. "It's cold, but you should be warm enough in my jacket."

Ann didn't bother to argue. She slid her arms into the fleece-lined jacket.

"Are you ready to leave?"

A monumental question, she mused. She wavered, wanting to stay where it was safe. In a quick stride, she forced herself to step out the door.

Damp cold air blasted at her face. Soon she'd have answers, she hoped. On a long inhale, she smelled the air's freshness. Splashes of sunlight glistened on the dew clinging to leaves. A new day meant a new start.

Huddling deeper in the oversize jacket, she withdrew a hand from the pocket to accept the gloves Nick waved at her. Repeatedly he did something small and inconsequential, something caring. Before he rounded the Jeep, she reached out and touched his arm, halting him. "You can't keep being nice and not expect more thank-yous."

Deliberately Nick made light of her words. "I'll swear at you every once in a while to keep things even."

"Sounds fair," Ann said on a laugh.

It was a sound he hadn't heard once in the past few days. Sliding behind the steering wheel, he wished it grated on him. Some women had high-pitched cackles. Not her. She had a low husky laugh that enticed, that made a man imagine hearing it in his ear while they snuggled on the bed in darkness. As he flicked on the ignition, he considered that he might be going crazy from too much peace and quiet.

Fortunately, for the next half hour he was too busy to think about her. With the dirt road barely passable, the ride from the cabin was a bumpy one. Nick maintained a slow speed and a firm grip on the steering wheel.

Being jostled in her seat, Ann clutched the side of it. "How long is the ride on this?"

"Several miles."

Then they'd reach the highway. She had to ask the one question plaguing her. "Where are we going first?"

Nick kept his eyes on the road. Logic dictated their first step. "You're going to see a doctor."

A swell of uneasiness stormed her. "Why? I'm fine."

"I know you feel okay." Nick veered to the right to avoid a large pothole. "But it makes sense to see one."

Not for the first time, she wondered what usually happened to someone who had amnesia. Was it viewed as a mental illness? Shutting her eyes for a second, she tried to block that thought. Why did that one fear keep returning? Had she been in a mental institution? What if she'd escaped from one? No, that made no sense. She had to be logical and not emotional. She was well-dressed, manicured and not likely a patient anywhere. "Can I turn on the radio?" she asked, needing something to soothe her.

Nick heard nerves in her voice. "Go ahead."

As the lulling quality of "Beethoven's Ninth" drifted through the Jeep, she drew several deep breaths. Relax. You'll be okay. Giving up her viewing of the woods, she noted that he'd set his shoulder holster on the floor at his feet. "Was your family pleased when you became a policeman?"

Nick eyed the highway junction sign ahead. "My father visualized his boy taking over the restaurant when he retired." He considered his own words. "But everyone knows he'll never retire."

"Who's everyone?"

In his family, no one's birthday went without celebration. Family gatherings included more than birthday and holiday celebrations. Vincettis gathered for picnics and leaf raking and snowball fights. To them, family meant unity, always being there for each other. "Immediate family includes parents and two sisters, brothers-in-law and a niece," he said, while making the turn onto the paved highway.

Though Ann didn't know the people he'd talked about, she could imagine motherly and sisterly worry, and eventually parental pride. Did she have parents who cared about her, loved her? He'd talked about his sisters with such warmth. Were there siblings she felt that way about? She hoped so. When she learned her identity she hoped that she was loved. "Why can't I remember if I have a family?"

Nick had wondered that, too. The idea of ever forgetting his family seemed so improbable that he couldn't imagine it happening. They were everything to him. "You're not ready to remember them."

If a family exists, Ann mused. "Tell me about your sisters. Are they younger?"

"Both of them." Nick followed her lead for small talk. "Bianca always played mother hen and bossed Mara and me around. She's known for being the double *N*. Nosy nag."

His love for them seemed so obvious. "She's married?"

"She and Angelo got married over ten years ago. They wanted kids, and when it looked as if that would never happen, they decided to adopt. You can guess what happened. She got pregnant. She's blossomed in the last few months but looks good."

Ann noted so much pride as he talked. "Your other sister—Mara—she's the youngest?"

"Right. She got married last March. She has a daughter, Jessie, not his. Though you wouldn't know it. Rick's more of a father to Jessie than the jerk Mara had been married to."

It was, she decided, in her favor that protective instincts came naturally to him. "How did they meet?"

"At a garbage can. She was taking out the trash and suddenly went into labor with Jessie, and Rick had to take her to the hospital. Romantic, huh?"

"Actually, it is," she said softly. It was romantic to find a man who'd come to the rescue when a woman needed someone the most.

"She's just learned that she's pregnant again." The first signs of civilization came into view. "So is anything familiar?"

Ann took several deep breaths to uncoil the knot in her stomach and focused on a gas station general store. Had she seen it before, been on this highway? "I don't remember seeing any of this." A chill slipping over her, she flicked up the heater switch and angled one vent toward her. She hoped she would learn she was a strong woman, confident, successful, well liked. Was that too much to hope for?

Head bent, she rezipped the parka. The warmth of the lining cocooned her, but she shivered. Every mile closer to the city meant a head-on collision with the unknown. Though she planned to stand on her own feet, she couldn't immediately, and that meant asking something of him. She knew this moment had to come, but despite the time she'd spent considering it, she felt immense discomfort. "Will you help me?" she blurted before she changed her mind.

Nick had never considered otherwise. "I'll help."

She leveled nerves. She needed more from him. "Would you promise something?"

To him, promises were sacred. Frowning, Nick wondered where this conversation was going. "What is it?"

"Will you tell me the truth? No matter what you learn, promise you won't lie to me."

Nick could imagine no reason for such a request except someone had lied to her, had hurt her with deception. He didn't ask. He doubted she knew why she'd asked that of him, but it seemed vital to her well-being. "Of course." He made another promise, a silent one, the kind he hoped someone would make if one of his sisters were in her place. He wouldn't desert her. Before he walked away, she would have her life back.

"No cranial concussion," the doctor at the emergency room assured her. Young and rushed, he ran a hand across tired-looking eyes, then stared at the clipboard in his hands as if double-checking his notes. "You need a follow-up visit with your own physician though."

Ann had no idea who that was. And what would another doctor tell her? She'd gone through a battery of tests and, at Nick's insistence, fingerprints had been taken.

"Well, you appear to be in perfect physical condition. So all I can do is assure you that it's probably temporary amnesia."

How temporary? she wondered. Would she know

her name by the end of the day, a week, a month from now?

Head bent, the doctor gave his notes another glance. "In the meantime, until you find your family, we have facilities here for people in your situation."

He aroused Ann's worst fear. "For how long?" she asked, astonished she sounded so calm.

"She has a place to stay," Nick said, without thinking beyond the moment.

Ann wanted to weep with relief.

Appearing harried, the doctor looked equally relieved to have the problem off his hands. "I'll take this release form to the admittance desk. Sign it before you leave."

"Nick, I don't know what to say," Ann said, the moment they were alone. A thank-you seemed too simple to convey the enormity of emotion she felt.

"You asked me to help." Before she could say more, Nick swung away. "I have to make a phone call." Bringing her into his home might be a mistake. Only once had he acted impulsively, had desire for a woman hit him so hard and fast that he'd tossed away reasoning. In a few short days, he'd felt the same swift attraction for this woman.

But whether he wanted to or not, he needed to think like a cop. Not only did she have another life somewhere, but also, quite possibly, another man existed, waiting and worrying about her. And there could be complications with her so near. He countered his own thought. No, he wouldn't let there be. Bottom line was that this was destined to be a short-term relationship. As long as he didn't forget that, they would be okay.

Digging into his pocket for coins, he stopped by a public phone. If he phoned his partner, Riley might secure information by the time Nick reached his house. It made sense that the sooner he got her where she belonged, the better.

Since it was early evening, he assumed his partner had sneaked downstairs to the vending machine for a candy bar. Though growing more impatient, Nick waited.

"Garrison, Homicide," Riley finally answered.

"Stuff your face and listen," Nick said.

"Whoa, wait a minute. Where are you calling from?"

"That's not important. I'm headed home."

As expected, Riley tossed a gibe at him. "Couldn't you handle roughing it?"

"I had an unexpected guest."

"What are you talking about?"

"It's a long story. I need you to do something for me. Scan missing persons data for a female, approximately twenty-seven, blond, green eyes, five foot eight, around 115 to 120 pounds—a looker. She probably disappeared during the last week."

"Your guest?" he asked between chews.

"Yeah." In a few short sentences, he filled Riley in on what had happened to Ann. "I'll call you back from home."

His home, a shingled bungalow, was nothing like Ann had expected. It was middle-class America. It was the kind of place people bought to raise children.

His keys in hand, Nick caught her arm when they reached the loose top step. Beneath moonlight, her face was bathed in shadows, making him want to strain closer to see it better. "Don't expect much. It's an old house, 1907 or something like that." He unlocked the door. "It included a low price tag and plenty of repairs."

Stepping into the foyer ahead of him, Ann viewed the living room's low-beam ceiling and brick fireplace and what looked like the original light fixtures of hammered copper and amber glass. She thought the house was wonderful. While he riffled through a stack of mail, she crossed the wood floor and entered the living room to get a better look at a built-in plate rail and a bookcase. In midstride, she stopped. A flimsy excuse for a bra dangled over the arm of the sofa near a backpack.

Clutching the food bag, she wandered back to the entrance hall and followed him into the kitchen. She'd misinterpreted everything. What she'd thought was attraction had been kindness. And so filled with gratitude, she'd made too much of his every look. Well, she wouldn't anymore. She would eat, but then she was leaving. She knew if she asked him whether she would be in the way, because of his kindness, he would deny it even if that were true.

"Go ahead and start." With a glance at the clock on the wall above the stove, Nick set the other food bag on the table. "I have a phone call to make."

Sighing, Ann sank to the closest chair. In the

kitchen, she felt more warmth. Shiny copper pots hung above the stove. The table with captain chairs was located near a bay window. She felt comfortable, too comfortable. She couldn't give in to what she wanted. He didn't deserve to have her turn his world topsy-turvy. Even now, she could hear him talking on the telephone in the living room. Feeling lousy, she nibbled at a French fry. Was he telling some woman he couldn't see her tonight? Be fair to him. Don't weaken.

At the sound of footsteps, she kept her head bent while she unwrapped the greasy wrapper around her sandwich.

"Sorry I took so long." Nick straddled a chair and fished into a bag for a French fry. "I had to make two calls." One was about her. Riley had proved reliable as usual and had cajoled some woman at missing persons to get answers for him. Those answers were Ann's business. Rising, he crossed to the refrigerator and withdrew a beer, aware he was stalling. He'd never liked playing the messenger with bad news. As a cop, he'd done it often enough and had never hardened himself completely to others' sadness.

"Could I have one of those?"

To keep the door from closing, he cupped his fingers over the top of it. "You want a beer?" he asked with surprise.

"Is that a problem?"

"If I hunt around, I might find a bottle of white wine somewhere."

Thoughtfully Ann stared at him. "Do you think I'd prefer that?"

"What I think isn't important. It's your choice. For now, you have more than most people." He retrieved the wine bottle, but set the beer in front of her. "Go ahead and try it."

"Why won't I have them later?" she asked, before taking a quick swallow from the beer can.

As she wrinkled her nose, Nick stifled a grin and poured the wine into a fluted glass. "Because no one does," he said, offering her the glass. "I could never turn my back on my family, so that's not a choice, is it?"

Ann sipped the wine and acknowledged he'd been right. She preferred the wine's smooth, mellow taste. Choices. She'd given that idea little thought. But if she couldn't find any family, she would have to start a new life. Her mind raced with new thoughts. "I could make up a last name. Get a job and a place to live."

Mentally Nick rejected the plan. Alone, she would really be lost. "You're going to do all that with no identification? Wouldn't it be better to find your family?"

"Isn't the question really something else? Is there a family?"

How could he answer that? Nick wondered. Maybe she didn't have anyone.

"And what if I never find out? What if I'm one of those Jane Does? I'd have to pretend I'm someone else. Start over."

Nick knew better. He'd learned the hard way that people couldn't change who they were. Trying to fit in to Julia's world had been a waste of time and effort. But what could he say? For all he knew, she might never find out who she was or reunite with someone who knew her. She might never feel the security of memories that most people took for granted. "Are you up to some news?" Nick asked between the last bites of his hamburger.

Ann swallowed the wine in her mouth. His brow had furrowed, an indicator that it wasn't good news. Well, she would face it. She would deal with anything that came her way. She really had no other choice. "What did you learn?"

From experience, Nick knew that the best way to deliver bad news was quickly. "No one with your description has been reported missing."

She visibly folded, as if all the strength she'd gathered had slithered away.

Nick stared into dull eyes. She looked so lost, so alone, but he offered no sympathetic words. He'd already noted she was straightening her back as if someone had punched it. Joan of Arc would have palled in comparison for bravery. "So no one reported you missing. That doesn't mean—"

"If you're loved, you're missed."

At the sadness hanging in her voice, he hunched forward. No thought went into his actions. Her hand was near on the table, pale and soft and slender. "You don't think you're loved?" he asked quietly, closing his fingers over hers.

Difficult words stuck in her throat for a moment. "I don't know."

"I think you are."

The brush of his knuckle across her cheek brought her head up.

"The doctor said this was temporary." He wanted to give her more and couldn't.

Ann had viewed that comment as standard spiel from a doctor to someone with memory loss. "Should I believe him?"

Her skepticism came through clearly. What had made her lack faith in others? "Tomorrow might be better." Those sounded like empty words even to him, but he couldn't offer any real reassurances. "If you're ready, I'll show you to your room."

Ann didn't give herself time to consider what she would face if she left his home. She only knew that imposing on him was unfair, that she had no right to disrupt his life-style. "I've decided not to stay," she announced to his back.

Baffled barely described the emotion Nick felt. Pausing at the kitchen doorway, he shot a look at her. "Where are you going to go?"

In that second, she knew only one option remained open to her. "The doctor said they had facilities."

Something wasn't right here, Nick decided instantly. Eyes, dark and shadowed with troubled thoughts, had raised to him when the doctor had made the suggestion. He'd seen her fear. "I thought you didn't want to go there."

Her stomach churned just from considering a stay at the mental facilities. But her worries, her problems weren't his. "I changed my mind."

"It's too late to leave," he said firmly. Not for the

first time, he admitted that women weren't always easy to understand.

Ann considered protesting, but logic prevailed. Despite what she'd said to him, she didn't plan on going back to the hospital. If she left now, she'd be wandering alone at night. That bordered on stupid. So she'd stay for tonight. "Only tonight," she insisted.

For the moment, Nick didn't force the issue. "If that's what you want."

Ann trailed him up the stairs. At the second floor, in passing, she viewed a room loaded with weight-lifting equipment. What the house lacked in decor, it made up for in charm, with carved moldings and stained glass.

"Here." Nick opened a door for her. "I'll get some towels and a T-shirt for you."

The room she stepped into contained a bed, a bed-side table with a lamp and a secondhand dresser, but the patchwork quilt and an ancient-looking steamer trunk gave the room a homey look. Curious of the view, she crossed to the window. With a look down, she saw that a huge willow, lightly dusted with snow, held center stage in the backyard.

Behind her, Nick paused at the doorway. He liked the way she moved with a fluid ease. He liked the proud straightness of her back, the lift of her chin. He liked too damn much about her. Quietly he moved within feet of her, even as he sensed the need for distance. Too often he found himself wanting to pull her into his arms. He couldn't kid himself. Comforting her only edged the need churning within him.

"How about returning a favor to me," he said, stopping an arm's length from her.

Ann whirled around and looked up from the T-shirt dangling in his hand. Eyes, intense and searching, met hers. "What favor?"

"Tell me why you changed your mind about staying here." As he spoke, he tried to remember when that had happened. She'd been pleased with his home, even curious. She'd wandered into the living room and... Nick tossed the T-shirt onto the bed. This reversal had started after her trip to the living room.

This was worse than Ann had imagined. She didn't want to have to explain. What could she say? *I know there's no wife, but is there a woman who feels you belong to her? Will she mind that you're helping me?* After the foolishness she'd uttered last night, if she asked him about his love life, he would think she was making a move on him. She had little choice, she realized. "If I stay, I'll be interfering."

Nick didn't give an inch. "Why?" Overhead light suddenly caught the glow of her hair. "Because of what you saw in the living room?"

"I told you." Uneasy, Ann breathed deeply. "I don't want to interfere with anything."

"I've been straight with you before this, haven't I." Nick demanded more than asked. "My cousin was staying here. He's lousy at picking up after himself." Over the phone, he'd leveled a few choice words at Carmen. "Does knowing that settle the problem?"

Ann pretended interest in the patchwork quilt. "No." He'd cleared up her misconception, but that didn't change what seemed obvious. She'd be in the way. "If there's someone special in your life, she might not like me being here."

She was sweet. It was the first thought that had leapt to his mind. It wasn't the last. At some moment, he'd moved closer. He'd known he would. If she'd moved away, he wouldn't have stopped her, but she didn't. It was all the encouragement he needed. For hours, he'd wanted to feel her body snug against his again. And he'd wanted more. A lot more. Soft, bare of lipstick, her lips invited him as it had for days. "There isn't anyone," he murmured, before he lowered his mouth and tasted her.

Ann had expected heat. She'd anticipated it. But when his mouth slanted across hers, she knew nothing in her imagination would have prepared her for this. Warmth seeped through her. The mouth on hers delivered a message of power, persuasion, seduction. As his tongue touched and dueled with hers, she curled her fingers into the material of his shirt. She'd wanted to know how she would respond to a kiss. Now she no longer cared if there had been others before him.

She drifted with the excitement, the emotion, the heat. She melted beneath the sensation slithering through her and strained against him, her mouth hard on his, her tongue meeting the challenge of his. She felt the length and heat of him. She felt desire within him—and her. With a need so strong that its ache curled inside her. She clung, wanting the moment to go on, wanting to feel more, even as she needed to catch her breath, even as he began to draw away.

With effort, Nick loosened his embrace. He'd been

close, too close, to racing his hand down her lean
body. One quick kiss was all he'd planned. He'd
meant to make a point, meant to end the fascination
that had started days ago, then her slender body had
swayed into his and the softness of her lips had answered his. Desire still warming him, he fought himself to keep from reaching out for her again. With her
breath hot on his face, he struggled to think. The possibility she might feel regret later shadowed the moment. "But what about you?" he asked, speaking
with as much steadiness as he could muster.

Color drained from her face. Nick couldn't let it
touch him. If he did, they wouldn't walk away from
each other again. He wouldn't let them.

Chapter Five

Unlike any others, his question still haunted Ann when she awakened the next morning. His words had washed over her as if a bucket of cold water had been tossed at her. Could she feel so much in one man's arms, if another existed? Desire hadn't seemed unfamiliar to her. She'd wanted to stay in his arms. She'd wanted him to keep kissing her. Would she have felt so much so quickly if she were accustomed to man-woman game playing? She didn't think she was some sexual seductress. She doubted, too, that she was a virgin. She was in her late twenties and not uncomfortable in a male embrace. Was that because of another man? Or was it because of Nick?

Sighing, she wandered into the bathroom. Maybe because she was too keyed up, she was susceptible to the slightest emotion. How could she possibly trust her feelings for him? How could she be sure of anything, even a dream that had awakened her in the middle of the night? A dream of shadows and movement. A winding staircase, a ringing phone—a key. And muffled voices.

Disgusted with her inability to interpret anything from that, she yanked her washed panties and bra from the shower curtain rod. For now, she would have to make do. Dressed in jeans and one of Nick's denim shirts, she rolled up the sleeves while moving around the room, hunting for the boots she'd shed without thought last night. The gray hint of morning only edged the sky. She located one boot under the dresser; the other hid beneath the bed.

While she tugged on her boots, she faced her own future. She couldn't be in limbo any longer, waiting moment to moment for some breakthrough. She needed to make a life for herself. The possibility that her memory might never return had hit her while being examined by the doctor in the emergency room. She'd even convinced herself during a rare optimistic second that some people might consider her lucky. She was being given a chance to start over, to reinvent her life.

Moving to the sink, she finger-brushed her teeth. Why hadn't she thought of a toothbrush last night? Amazing. With all that was wrong in her life, all she might materialistically yearn for, she wanted a toothbrush most of all.

She turned off the water and listened for Nick's singing. She heard nothing then, or when she strolled to the kitchen. And she missed him. That might be her biggest mistake. With no idea what the future would bring, she needed to control her emotions. She really didn't have any room in her life for soft dreamy notions about him, about any man. If she was wise she'd forget the kiss, think about herself, who she was, her future.

For the next few minutes, she puttered around the kitchen, setting the table, pouring juice. Yesterday she'd watched Nick closely, noting how much water went into the coffeemaker, how many scoops of ground coffee beans belonged in the basket. She finished the task and was plugging in the brewer when she heard the back door opening.

Pivoting, she met him with a bright smile. "Good morning. I made coffee," she announced. Uncertain of his mood, she kept busy at the counter. "Where have you been?"

Breathing hard, Nick stripped off his jacket. "Running." And thinking. She looked lovely, standing in the glow of the morning sunlight. She looked like a coed with her hair back and secured with some kind of hair thing his sister had left at his house.

Growing edgier with his silence, Ann fingered the white bow clip in her hair. "I used this. Was that all right?" When she'd seen it on the dresser, she'd wondered who it belonged to and had hesitated using it. According to him, no special woman existed in his life, but she doubted he'd lived like a monk. No man who smiled like that, who kissed like that, was alone often.

"It's okay." He knew her taste now; it wouldn't be easy to forget. Nothing was okay, not really. More than desire was drawing him to her. "It's Mara's," he answered before turning away in response to the ringing phone. For distance from her as much as for privacy, he strolled to the living room instead of picking up the kitchen phone.

Ann settled on the window seat near the bay window. Whenever his eyes met hers, the memory of one kiss seemed to whisper on the air. With a look, he could make her blood warm. With a kiss, he'd flamed that heat. It still simmered within her, and he'd left the room seconds ago.

Spotting a snow shovel against the porch railing, Ann reacted instinctively. It took only minutes to hunt up the necessary clothing. As she opened the door, the cold stunned her.

Nick finished the call, muttering to himself and preparing to play messenger again. Mulling over what Riley had told him, he returned to the kitchen. She'd disappeared. He considered another cup of coffee, but the scrape of a shovel led him to the window. Snow fell swiftly, covering the ground in white. He saw her struggling against the wind, tossing shovels of snow to the side. Releasing a lusty oath, he grabbed his jacket and stormed out the door. "Go inside. It's too cold," he yelled over the wail of the wind.

The coldness hurting her lungs, to catch her breath, Ann stilled. Though freezing, she mentally balked at what had sounded like an order.

Through a blurry haze of snow, Nick slitted his eyes at her. He caught the stubborn lift of her chin and gave up. If this was where she wanted him to break the news, so be it. "Wisconsin authorities called." Her eyes snapped in his direction. Within them was a yearning, a greediness to be told something, anything, about her past. "They found a Porsche with Illinois plates."

Hope rushed through her, penetrating every pore. "So I am from here?" She racked her mind to visualize such a car.

"It had a sticker on the window for one of the suburbs."

Her breath puffed on the freezing air. "Was there a purse?"

"Just a jacket." As if possessing a will of their own, his fingers caught wispy strands of hair flying across her cheek. "A fur-lined suede—worth a few thousand."

Her skin warming with his caress, she grappled to formulate another question. "No suitcase?"

Following her train of thought wasn't difficult. "You weren't on a planned trip."

As quickly as her optimism formed, it flowed out of her now. "Nothing is simple. If there had been a purse, a wallet, there would be identification."

No, nothing was simple, Nick mused. Until Monday he couldn't call the Motor Vehicles Department and get that identification from them. "I have to return Riley's Jeep. Want to go with me?"

Something unspoken passed between them. She said nothing, nodding, but he sensed they'd taken a step closer. He wanted her with him; she'd wanted to go. And for the first time in five years, he felt vulnerable, aware of a woman who could split him apart if he let her.

Ann settled in his car, unsure how to interpret this afternoon's outing. She wanted to believe he'd asked her because he liked being with her. Yet she forced herself to expect another sight-seeing trip.

What she never anticipated was finding herself inside a suburban shopping mall. Whether he meant to or not, he stunned her.

"Here." Nick dug his wallet from his back pocket and lifted bills from it. "You can't live in that outfit."

Surprise barely measured what she was feeling. It was one thing to accept his help, quite another to take money from him. Recovering quickly, she shoved his hand away. "I can't take that."

"Sure you can." Nick grinned. He'd tagged her as proud almost from the beginning, but he was trained at pushing the right buttons. "Take it. You might find out more about yourself."

Of course, she wanted to learn more about herself. He was a master at persuasion, Ann decided. Often he'd said or done something to make her face herself honestly. On a resigned sigh, she slipped the bills from him. "Thank you. I'll pay you back."

"When you can." Nick sensed the effort it had taken for her to make such a concession. "Let's find out what you like."

In minutes, she discovered that she loved to shop. She learned that she preferred dark colors or white. She liked basic tailored clothes, no frills or flounces or flowered patterns.

Hours later, dangling bags of clothes, she strolled with him toward the exit. He'd given her more than a wardrobe. Because of him, she suddenly owned more than the clothes she wore. To her, that symbolized a step forward.

Silent, she sat in the car and watched snowflakes dance in the air as they drove along Lake Shore Drive. The cold, dark sky blended in with the choppy water of the lake. Buildings of white marble, stainless steel and tinted glass rose toward the sky. All of it seemed familiar. Because of what he'd told her, because she was from here? she wondered. Or because she was fooling herself into believing she remembered it? "Where are we going now?" she asked as she noticed he'd missed the turn toward his house. Whenever they'd been in the car, she'd keyed in on street names. Though none had been familiar, she'd memorized every one of them.

"I thought you might be hungry. This is the best place to eat in the city."

As he whipped the car into a parking space in front of a restaurant, Ann turned from reading the sign for Vincetti's and saw his grin. She laughed, but her emotions were scrambled. She was going to meet his family. He wouldn't have brought her here if he hadn't wanted her to. Trying to quiet her nerves, she walked with him toward the entrance.

Nick hunched against the chill and opened the door, hustling Ann inside. He was getting in too deep. He knew it yet couldn't stop himself.

The restaurant bustled with activity. Catering to Italian-Americans, it provided a gathering place for families. Nick set a hand at the small of Ann's back and urged her toward an unoccupied table for two in a far corner of the restaurant. In passing, he nodded his head to several regulars. He felt more than their attention following him and Ann.

"Nicholas!" His family's radar had clicked on.

Exuberant as ever, his Aunt Gina rushed over, opening fleshy arms to greet him.

While she gave him a sturdy hug, his mother weaved her way to them.

"We came to get something to eat." His last word trailed off as his father materialized, grinning.

Nick made introductions.

His sister didn't wait for one. Bianca eased onto a chair beside Ann. Over jeans and a bright yellow polo shirt, she wore a denim-colored apron that curved around the large mound at her midsection, emphasizing the last stage of pregnancy. "I'm Bianca."

Ann rushed forward a smile. "Hi."

Nick caught his family's puzzled looks at his omission of Ann's last name, but diverted everyone's attention to Bianca. "Pay no attention to her," he told Ann. "We're sure someone dropped her on her head at an early age."

"Cute." With practiced ease, Bianca ignored him. "Mara, come help me," she called.

"My other sister. This is Mara," Nick said to Ann.

"Nice meeting you, Ann." Her dark eyes flashing with humor, his youngest sister nudged him with an elbow. "I thought you were going fishing." She sniffed exaggeratedly. "You don't smell as bad as you usually do when you come back from those trips. Why aren't you playing Daniel Boone?''

"Plans change."

Bianca took over and drilled the next question at him. "So how did you two meet if you were in some wilderness in Wisconsin?"

Ann made much about working out of her jacket. Let him handle that question.

"In some wilderness in Wisconsin," Nick quipped for an answer.

With perfect timing to save him from a lengthy explanation, his mother played rescuer. "Bianca, I could use help in the kitchen."

She tsked. "Honestly, Mama. How will we find out anything about her if I don't sit here?" Before she swung away, she touched Ann's shoulder as if they were old friends.

"She's nice," Ann commented, smiling.

"*Nosy* sounds more accurate to me," Nick said with affection.

"And your other sister is really beautiful."

He knew that was true. But there were different kinds of beauty. While Mara was flash and darkness, Ann possessed a warm blond fairness.

Through the meal, he watched her. Tension seemed to ooze away. He'd hoped for this. As he'd expected, family members repeatedly wandered back to their table, and with each visit, she relaxed more. Nick rested a hand on the back of her chair, liking the way her laughter rose on the air. He'd wanted to see her like this, calm, her eyes bright, her face glowing.

* * *

"I feel mellow," Ann murmured when Nick braked the car on the driveway beside his house. How wonderful it had been to enjoy herself, to feel almost normal. "What was that dessert called?" she asked when she started up the steps to the porch with him.

With a subtle shift of his body, Nick blocked her from the cold air. *"Mousse di cioccolato."*

The creamy white chocolate mousse had awakened taste buds she'd been unaware of. "Did you really leave your sister at a neighbor's and tell them to keep her?"

Nick chuckled softly, recalling the disbelief that had flashed over her face when Bianca had told the story. "I was four," he said in his defense.

Laughing, she looked up. "I had a good time," she said on a breath not quite steady. She tried to smile and couldn't. Emotion skittered through her. He was looking at her again as if no other woman existed. Tilting her head, she made the first move this time, bringing her lips a hairbreadth from his.

Air, cold and harsh, battered Nick's back. But with her lips against his, he knew only her warmth and sweetness. He heard a soft sound, a moan that fueled him. He'd made love to some women and had felt less than he did from a kiss with her. Again he wanted to drown himself in her taste. He wanted to drive her senseless, even as he struggled to remember that she was caught up in a world of unknowns.

Then she strained against him, too eager, too needy. Craving, he didn't care why she was responding. The longing, the urgency was with him again. She tasted as wonderful as before. As he deepened the kiss, as his tongue slipped into the warm dark recesses of her mouth, for this moment, only sensations mattered. He absorbed all that she offered, all that fogged thoughts. Pressing against her, he damned clothes. He wanted to bury himself in her.

Aching, he ran his lips over her face, his mind wandering with fantasies of caressing her, of tasting the womanly scent of her flesh. She was touching something beyond passion within him. But what was he doing to her? She didn't need him jumbling her thoughts. It took effort to think that much. "I've never taken advantage of a woman," he said roughly, pulling away. "I don't plan to start now."

The words sounded more like a reminder to himself than for her benefit. Still reeling, breathless, Ann wondered how he could say that, how he expected her to agree when the softness in his voice swirled around her like a warm caress. Did he imagine she would pretend that hadn't happened? That she would forget the kisses shared, the excitement? She'd wanted him to kiss her again, to detonate feelings inside her. A fierce tug tempted her to sway close even now and ease the throbbing inside her. "You have a short memory," she said unsteadily.

Unlocking the door, Nick rounded a puzzled look over his shoulder at her.

"I kissed you," Ann reminded him, then passed him in the doorway. Not looking back, she climbed the stairs to her room.

Two days passed, two days of too many times that their hands brushed when they both reached for something, too many times of a look passing between them that carried a reminder of the last kiss, too many times when they stood too close and desire clung to the air.

Even Nick's efforts to keep everything casual failed. Despite the noise and brightness in the bowling alley last night, her laughter over a gutter ball had slithered over him with a heat that made him feel like some kid with an overactive libido.

He awoke before dawn with intentions of making an early call to the Motor Vehicle Department about the owner of the Porsche. On the way to the spare room to exercise, he convinced himself nothing would happen again.

Then he saw her in the hallway, bathed in a glow of the morning sunlight. Strands of her hair shone like sun-kissed silk. With it messed from sleep, she delivered a dreamy, half-awake smile. His eyes roamed to the slim, strong legs revealed below the hem of his T-shirt. Annoyed, he pulled his gaze back to her face. On the way, he skimmed the cloth clinging to her breasts and hips. As his blood heated, he wanted to step forward, drag her against him. But the more she gave, the more he'd want. Even now, her taste still lingered, haunting him. So he didn't move.

''I'll be in the kitchen in a minute.'' Ann thought he'd mumbled a response. She wasn't sure of anything as she stared at the muscles rippling in his naked back. He didn't really have to say anything. She'd noticed that look, the same one that had darkened his eyes an instant before they'd kissed. More than once, he'd awakened desire within her. Because of him, she knew now what it was to long for a touch, for the heat of a kiss—his kiss. She sensed he wasn't happy about what had happened, and she didn't understand the quickness of it. But it was back again, strong and potent and enticing.

Perhaps she was a little mad. Wasn't it insane to feel so much so quickly for another person? Did she always rush impulsively into relationships? Was she easy?

In the bathroom, Ann washed her face. Days had passed since she'd lost her memory, yet the woman in the mirror remained a stranger to her. It seemed ridiculous that she didn't know a blessed thing about herself, yet she was welcoming such raw need for Nick. Was it lust or more? Was she clinging to the only person she felt linked to? Frowning, she spread toothpaste on a finger and wiped it over her teeth hard, twice, before she remembered she had a tooth-brush now.

In bra and panties, she rushed because of the cold and yanked on a new yellow turtleneck and tugged up her jeans. The new clothes brightened her spirits. Had she always felt that way? she wondered when strolling into the kitchen.

With time alone, she let her gaze roam over a sports calendar; the month of December featured a skier. On the kitchen counter was a glass jar that had snagged her interest yesterday. It was filled with an odd as-sortment of what looked like junk—a matchbook from Las Vegas, marbles, coins, keys, a plastic toy from a cereal box, a child's sheriff's badge, a wom-an's cheap pin, a tarnished silver necklace, a plastic house from a Monopoly game. "A keepsake jar of junk,'' she declared on a laugh, rotating it. Did she collect anything? She was beginning to feel as if she'd been born an adult on a rainy night in the Wisconsin woods.

Stepping away, she poured coffee, then stood for several seconds by the window, just enjoying the sight of the fresh, unmarred blanket of snow on the ground. On a yawn, she turned away. A sound, a faint meow, swung her around. Certain she hadn't imagined the sound, Ann veered toward the back door and opened it. Sitting, a black cat with one white front paw stared up at her. "Aren't you sweet? Want some milk?"

Not even exercise helped. In his bedroom, Nick rowed in time with Garth Brooks singing out a hand-clapping gospel song. He believed she'd felt the same need he had during that kiss. Nothing made sense. He didn't jump into relationships without thought—at least, he hadn't since Julia had swept in and out of his life. He had enough reasons to keep from getting too close to her. But all the reasoning in the world didn't stop him from wanting her in his arms again.

Slowing his pace, he blew out several long breaths. Oh, hell. He needed to stop thinking like a fool. He already had a clue to her background. An expensive car. By the end of the day, he'd know who that car belonged to.

Sweating, he dabbed a towel at his face as he pushed to a stand. In the meantime, he'd give Ann what she needed—security and compassion—and not what he wanted—her.

His mind full of her, he stepped out of the room, listening for the sound of her movements. When silence greeted him, he wandered downstairs, expecting to find her in the kitchen. She wasn't there. He returned to the stairs and walked through the second-floor hallway, opening and closing doors. Now where had she gone?

She wouldn't leave. For all her courage about not letting her situation depress her, she'd hardly venture out alone. She knew no one.

Returning to the kitchen, he heard a distinct sound outside his back door and flung it open. Squatting, Ann was pouring milk into a bowl for the cat.

Startled, she shot to a stand. "You scared the daylights out of me."

Content, the cat lapped away at the milk.

"Don't feed it," Nick insisted.

Considering all he'd done for her, she'd never have taken him for the hard-hearted type. "She has no home. And she's so adorable," Ann added with a look down at the cat.

"He. It's a *he*."

Leaning over, Ann stroked the furry back. "You don't like him?"

"He keeps dropping mice on my back porch."

Amusement coursed through her. He apparently knew nothing about cats, except one had ruined a Christmas for him, but she did. Was that because she owned a cat? "He loves you," she said in the cat's defense. "He's bringing you gifts."

"Wonderful."

She had the good sense not to say more, but

cracked a smile after he'd closed the door behind him. "Don't worry."

The cat purred as if he understood.

"He grumbles at me sometimes, too." She tucked a finger behind the cat's ear and scratched. "That means he likes you."

Time away from her, that's all he needed, Nick decided. Within half an hour, he'd entered the precinct and was strolling down the hall that had been painted an institutional green. He planned to get answers. He had to before everything got out of hand between them. Once she knew her name, this, whatever this was, would end simply. They'd go in different directions.

The noise in the squad room was a combination of ringing telephones and clicking keyboards blended in with laughter and a few curses.

In passing another detective's desk, Nick swiped a chocolate-covered doughnut from the box he brought in every day.

"I thought you'd gone on vacation."

"Couldn't miss getting my doughnut." Grinning, Nick chomped down on it and weaved his way around desks.

"Figured you'd last less than a week in the quiet woods with no excitement," another detective gibed.

Nick responded with an appropriate gesture and kept walking toward his desk. No excitement. That was good for a laugh. One woman had whisked into his life, bringing plenty of excitement with her.

Yawning, his partner was raking fingers through

tawny-colored hair. It was long again, nearly shoulder length. Sporting a beard, he'd recaptured his blond Serpico look, something he'd developed during too many years in vice. With his suede cowboy boots propped on his desk, he swiveled his chair toward Nick and gave him a wry boyish grin, one that Nick had seen buckle a few women's knees. "She staying with you?"

Nodding, Nick riffled through a few messages on his desk, one from a guy not known as being a reliable snitch.

"You should take her to your mother's house."

Nick quipped, "Is that your worldly wisdom for today?"

"Which you're going to ignore."

"You got it."

Riley gave him a stupid, taunting grin. "I talked to the shrink here. Just sort of inquired about amnesia."

"And what did she say?" He hoped some clinical information would make it easier for him to understand what Ann was going through, what she might still have to face.

"She rattled off a lot of stuff about nonpsychotic syndrome and—"

"What's that?"

"Stress. Something happens to a person that's too much to deal with." Riley dropped his feet from the desk. "Rage can cause it. And fear."

That one bothered Nick. He wasn't sure if someone was after her.

"Or humiliation. But since she hit her head, it might be posttrauma amnesia."

"Any idea how long it will last?"

"Who knows?" Riley fingered a report in front of him. "I have a message for you."

Chapter Six

Armed with detergent and a basket of dirty laundry, Ann ventured into the basement. For a long moment, she eyed the washing machine. Was this another first? Had she ever done laundry before or was her hesitancy about pushing buttons the result of her amnesia? Not wanting to flood the house, she hunted for the instructions to operate the washer. A few minutes later, she listened with satisfaction to the sound of water filling the machine.

Now she'd tackle the coffeemaker. She might not know her way around a kitchen, but she had grasped how to make a good cup of coffee. She ladled ground beans into the basket and reached for the plug.

"Don't plug it in."

The smile for Nick curving her lips never formed. Tension knotted the pit of her stomach at the seriousness she saw in his eyes. "You've found out more, haven't you?"

"For a man who can't find matching socks most mornings, Riley is thorough at investigating," Nick said with a trace of admiration. "Before he'd had a chance to check with the Motor Vehicles Department, Riley had gotten an old girlfriend to trace the license plate and car ownership records. I have a name." One that had told him what he'd suspected.

Ann clung by her fingertips against panic. As much as she'd yearned to learn her name, she was frightened of coming face-to-face with her identity.

"Gillian Somerset." Nick saw no flicker of recognition from her, even though Somerset was a well-known name on the society pages. Highbrow, they came from a circle of people who liked to stay with their own kind. Often enough, Julia's father had pointed that out to him.

Slowly Ann repeated the name; it meant nothing to her. "Is that my name?"

"Could be."

"Wouldn't it be?" She frowned, wondering why he was doubting what seemed a fact. "If Gillian Somerset owns that car and if I had it, then wouldn't that mean I'm her?"

More than ever, Nick thought they needed sound reasoning. "Or you borrowed her car."

Feeling even more lost, Ann averted her gaze. Of course, that was a possibility. Wouldn't that explain, too, why the name had triggered no recollection?

"I have an address." Nick fished a slip of paper

from his shirt pocket. "Want to take a ride to the apartment?"

Ann stretched for a deep breath. "I suppose so."

The nerves in her voice tugged at him. To hell with what he felt. She needed someone. She needed comfort. Stepping close, he slid his arms around her waist and protectively enveloped her.

"Even if I'm not her, if she loaned me her car, then she probably could identify me," she said, forcing hope in her voice. Stalling, she looked out the window at a sky dark and heavy with clouds. "It's late. Shouldn't we wait until tomorrow morning?"

He saw indecision in her face, as if she were warring a private emotional battle. "Listen to me—"

"I don't want to."

With the caution and gentleness of touching something breakable, Nick framed her face with his hands. She looked younger, vulnerable. "Now or later." Tenderly he kissed her brow. She needed to come to terms with the world of Gillian Somerset. So did he, he reminded himself, even as he pressed his cheek against hers. "It has to be done."

With her address tucked into the pocket of his peacoat, Nick drove toward the high-class apartments near the heart of Michigan Avenue shopping. When she regained her memory, he wouldn't fit in. It amazed him that he needed to keep reminding himself of that. He'd walked a similar path before with a woman.

At the double glass door of the high rise, a gray-haired doorman smiled at Ann from the other side.

With no hesitation, he unlocked the door, then opened it. "Good evening, Ms. Somerset."

So that's me. Her heart pounding, Ann returned a weak smile. A cowardly streak coursing through her, she doubted she'd have taken another step. It was the gentle pressure of Nick's hand at her back that nudged her forward. She led the way past the man to an elevator, but steps from it, she balked. "Which floor? Which apartment?" she murmured low to Nick.

Nick had already considered this problem. "Guess it's time for some playacting. Open that purse you bought and pretend to look for your keys."

Minutes later, he decided that she should have moonlighted onstage. That bothered him. Julia, too, had been accomplished at fooling people, especially him.

"Lots of people lose keys," the doorman assured her while accompanying them in the elevator to the penthouse apartment.

After he unlocked the apartment with a master key, Ann stated the obvious. "I'll need another set of keys made."

"I'll see to it, Ms. Somerset."

"Thank you. I'd appreciate that." She sounded calm, even managing a smile, but she must have appeared as terrified as she felt. Why else would the doorman give her such a strange look before he'd stepped away?

Standing behind her, Nick cupped hands on her arms and felt her tremble. He didn't doubt she was frightened. With the door open, she was steps from entering her world.

I'm not ready for this, Ann wanted to say. This was her home, but nothing looked familiar. She scanned the foyer, a wide entrance with white pillars, a marble floor, and a small round glass table with a black vase filled with tall twigs. It seemed so stark to her. "I must like trees but not flowers," she murmured with a nervous laugh.

"Take it one step at a time," he said quietly, urging her forward.

Hadn't she told herself that once before? But this moment seemed surreal to her. Silent, uneasy, she kept her hand in his, needing to maintain some contact with reality. She couldn't say she disliked the decor. From the all-white furniture and carpeting to the high-glossed ebony piano, the apartment carried a message of a sleek, sophisticated life-style. Walls of mirrors reflected expensive vases and statues in a wall-to-wall glass cabinet.

Nick forced the first step of many away from him. "Check out the other rooms."

Emotions tumbling together, Ann drew a sharp breath and meandered toward the bedroom. Stark white, it symbolized the personality of an obsessive perfectionist. A wall-to-wall walk-in closet revealed racks of expensive clothing that ranged from tennis outfits to designer gowns. She stared in awe. Was this all really hers? Had she spent every penny she had on clothes? More baffled now, she felt desperate for some link to the woman who lived here.

Inside a small top drawer of a desk, an Oriental

piece of ebony wood, she located a travel agency sheet listing a flight to Switzerland that was a year old. Beneath it, she found an invitation to a black-tie fund-raiser for a crisis organization, and a thank-you note about a hospital charity function. Is that how she spent her days? Traveling, participating in fund-raisers?

A survey of a dresser revealed that everything had a place, from expensive laced panties to silk scarves. A jewelry case was filled with gold and diamonds. Who are you? she wondered. Are you well liked, or merely tolerated? Kindhearted or selfish? Are you happy or lonely? She recalled the way the doorman had looked at her. He'd smiled when she'd politely thanked him for opening her apartment door, but he'd seemed what? Surprised? Confused? Why? Because she was rude or inconsiderate usually?

"Ann?" A shoulder braced against the doorjamb, Nick had followed her movements for several minutes. That lost look clouded her eyes again. "Come on." He wanted her near as much as he sensed she needed the closeness of another person. "I found a photo album."

Weary, she wished she was at his place. She wished— She stopped the thought as she paused beside the piano. Without forethought, she let her fingers dance across the keyboard. Why she'd stopped she couldn't say, but she set one hand and then the other on the keys. Lightly her fingers glided over keys with a lulling melody, a sequence of chords and finally a rush of notes. And she recognized the piece instantly as one of Bach's. "I can play the piano."

That was something tangible. She liked to play. No one needed to tell her. The second her fingers had touched the keyboard, she'd known.

For an instant, Nick saw a flicker of pleasure in her face. "Learn anything in the other room?" he asked when she settled beside him on the sofa.

Her possessions surrounded her. They could have belonged to someone else. She recognized none of them. "Enough to believe the apartment's occupant is unbelievably neat."

She sounded as uneasy now as the first night Nick had met her. Setting the leather photo album on her lap, he draped an arm around her shoulder. "These might help." He'd already gathered impressions. He'd viewed a painting, a Monet, but was unable to identify it as a copy or authentic. He'd scanned the bookshelves filled with editions of poetry that vied for space with books by Hemingway and Jane Austin, Ayn Rand, Rousseau and several books with French titles. When he'd removed one from the shelf, he'd fanned pages of foreign print. Clues were everywhere, from the books to the artwork to the classical CDs, perhaps not about why she'd forgotten this life but about the life-style she'd known.

Ann brushed her fingers across the leather album. It didn't feel familiar. She opened it and stared at the first photo. As if most important, it was a studio portrait of an elderly woman. Her gray hair neatly coiffured, she appeared small but regal looking. She also had warm bluish green eyes. Was this woman alive? Was she dear to her? An aunt? A grandmother?

"Does she look familiar?"

Head bent, she shook her head and turned a page. She had no time to prepare. Her breath hitched. An odd flutter attacked her stomach in response to photos of herself. In several of them, she was dressed in tennis shorts and a white top, her arm draped around the waist of a man who wore similar clothes. An inch or two taller than her, he was blond and tanned and handsome in an all-American looking way. Who was he to her? A brother? An old boyfriend? A cousin?

She perused several pages that revealed more photos of the man, of other strangers, most blond and well-dressed. Friends, she supposed.

Who was she really? She was in her world, yet as she'd explored it, she'd dealt with a sensation of invading the privacy of the woman who lived here. Gillian Somerset. Was that really her? As Nick shifted beside her, she closed the photo album. Would he leave now? The thought of being alone terrified her. In a deep part of her mind, she supposed she'd thought that the sight of familiar possessions would bring back memories. And that hadn't happened.

Linking her hand with Nick's, she saw questions in his eyes and looked for a way to avoid them. "We haven't had dinner. Do you want to see what we can find in the kitchen?"

Nick followed her lead. She was scared. More scared now than before. He nodded and wandered with her into the kitchen. Because of her cooking ability, or lack of it, he doubted they would find much food in her kitchen. He was right. The refrigerator contained a bottle of mineral water, a can of caviar and three wrinkled-looking oranges. A cupboard revealed a bottle of Scotch, crackers, a box of instant coffee and several cans of soda.

Ann forced a soft laugh. "Hardly the well-stocked kitchen of a woman who loves to cook." Aware of Nick's closeness behind her, she nearly swayed back against him. She wished for time to stop—right now, with his body so close to her. But reality swarmed in on her. The ticking of a wall clock was already snatching this moment away. The heavy, unbearable pressure building up in her chest intensified. He couldn't help her, not really. Alone, she'd have to walk the path back to her life, and each step would be difficult. "Let's go out."

Though just as eager to get her out of the sterile-looking apartment that lacked her warmth, he hesitated. He should break away now. Even before he'd known her name, he'd thought that whatever happened between them would be fleeting. He'd started out accepting responsibility for her. He'd rationalized feelings that had followed—sympathy, attraction, desire. Then as greater emotion had stirred for her, he'd cautioned himself, aware the more he got involved, the greater the risk. Only he hadn't listened. All the warnings had fallen on deaf ears. Taking her hand, he urged her toward the door. He suddenly felt as tugged in two directions as she did.

Instead of home, he drove her to a restaurant known for an ambience of soft lights and quiet. He thought it suited her mood. What she didn't need was noise and the buzz of conversation. Enough sights, too many thoughts were barraging her mind now.

Candlelight flickered between them, playing across her face. "What do you want?"

Closing the menu, Ann gave up any pretense with him. "It's strange what I'm feeling." Was it normal to feel so jumbled, so severed from everything that should have been familiar? "When we were at the cabin, I wanted so badly to find out who I was. Now I wish you hadn't told me."

Nick set down his wineglass. "You made me promise I would."

Ann gave her head a shake, as if trying to banish that memory. "Why did I?"

Lightly Nick stroked a thumb across the top of her hand. "You know why."

"Because I thought I needed to know," she said softly even as anger and frustration rose within her. "Why should that be so important? I could make new memories."

"You're smarter than that. The old ones would still be around," he reminded her.

By the time they had finished eating, Ann had see-sawed between moods so many times, she simply wanted to distance herself from her own thoughts. Stepping outside with him, she stared down at her feet as she ambled with him toward his car. Beneath a nearly full moon, the sheet of white on the ground glistened. "I like winter," she said. "The first snow-fall, the crisp, clean air." Knowing that meant more to her than the racks of clothes or sparkling jewelry or priceless art that she'd found in Gillian Somerset's apartment. No, my apartment, she reminded herself.

"I hope you don't like freezing, too," Nick grumbled on a shiver. "Let's—"

As he stopped talking, Ann raised her head and saw him staring in the direction of a limousine across the street. A tall blonde in a full-length fur had captured his attention. Ann wrestled with curiosity. She knew he collected silly trinkets, exercised daily, read thrillers and sang opera. She knew he was addicted to crossword puzzles, and cooked wonderfully. She knew she swam beneath shivers because of his kisses. But other than mentioning his divorce, he'd never spoken of the loves in his life. "She's beautiful," she commented with another glimpse back.

"Not so beautiful." He felt too much, Nick thought disgustedly. He loved too deeply. "That's my ex-wife."

Ann expected he'd say no more if she didn't prod. "Will you tell me about her?"

"It's the past."

"Your past. Not mine." She caught his arm, halting him with her. "Nick, I need to think about something else," she said almost desperately.

As a gust blew into his face, he lowered his head. Maybe it was time for her to realize what he'd ignored. With another woman, he'd already sampled the life they knew now that Ann belonged to, and he hadn't fit in. "When I was still in uniform, I was assigned to security at the Wainwright home. I don't know why anything between us went further, but it did." He remembered it as fast and furious with Julia. He'd had the same reaction to Ann. "Her family wasn't pleased. After we were married, her parents used every chance they got to tempt her with the wealth I couldn't offer her.'' Snow flew at his face. Angling it away, he met Ann's stare.

"Did your family like her?"

Nick added perceptiveness to her finer traits. As a couple approached on the sidewalk, he withdrew a hand from his pocket to link with hers and draw her closer. "You've met my family. They're not hard to like. They reach out to people. That's why the restaurant does so well. When they met her, they smiled at the right times and said the right things.''

"And that bothered you.''

It amazed him that in such a short time she knew him so well. "I thought if my family knew her better, they'd warm to her, so I suggested a night with them. She refused. She'd already made other arrangements that night.''

Having witnessed his closeness and affection for them, Ann imagined how much that must have hurt him. There was more, she guessed. Maybe some of it was too painful to share.

"In the end, she admitted that she missed the money.''

Ann couldn't imagine loving a man and letting something like money be more important. But who was she really?

A chill whipping through him, he said the obvious. "It's cold.''

When they reached the curb, Ann held back to still him again. "After your divorce, did your family tell you that they didn't like her?''

For the first time since he'd been reminiscing, a

hint of a smile edged his voice. "Never. They've never said a word against her."

Because they love him. "Nick, she..."

Head bent, he placed a gloved fingertip to her lips to silence her. "I don't want to talk about her."

Not all his scars had healed, Ann mused while she settled in the car beside him. Buckling her seat belt, she shifted several times to get comfortable. The last place she wanted to go was back to her apartment, a stranger's apartment. "Where are you taking me?"

"Wherever you want to go."

"Not there. I'm not ready to face all that again."

They drove to his home in silence. At the click of the front door lock, Ann preceded him inside. Only here, in his house, did she feel as if she belonged. She'd spent hours with him under this roof. She'd seen the way he looked first thing in the morning, his hair tousled. She'd watched the tiredness creep into his eyes at night. She knew him better than herself. "Nick, what if the memories aren't happy ones? What if forgetting everything and everyone was something I really wanted to do?"

"A lot of what-ifs." With his hands at her shoulders while he helped her with her coat, he nearly bent his head to seek the soft flesh at the curve of her neck. "What if you find out that you're missed, loved, that people are worrying about you? Would that make this easier?"

She swung around, facing him with an annoyed look that she knew he didn't deserve. "Aren't you ever afraid of what you don't know?"

"Sometimes." The sweet, clean scent of her pulled

at him again. He wanted to hold her, comfort her, love her. "Sometimes it's what we do know that we need to be more cautious around." He'd been reminding himself of that for days and still wasn't heeding his own advice.

"Well, I have a name and an apartment, and I still feel as if I'm disconnected. So maybe that's why I'm scared. It doesn't feel comfortable. I don't feel as if I belong there."

Nick cared too much about her to let the comment slide. "This will get easier." Lightly, almost hesitatingly, she set a hand at his waist, and he braced for sensation. Had any woman ever stirred him up so effortlessly? "The more you learn, the more you'll remember. No one has all bad memories, Ann. Trust me."

Didn't he know she had almost from the moment they met? "You sound so sure."

For her sake, he wished he felt that way. But it wouldn't get easier for him. He'd lost objectivity. He cared about her more than was wise.

Nick gave her time the next morning while he made waffles. But dodging anything wasn't his way. As a kid, he'd gone toe-to-toe with anyone rather than back off. She'd have a different life after today. Neither of them could change that. "What did you think of your apartment?" he asked while they ate, trying to ease her into conversation.

Ann met his gaze with a rebellious challenge. She'd hoped for at least the morning free of questions. "What did you think of it?"

Pricking a piece of waffle with his fork, Nick stifled a chuckle at the quick irritation he'd heard in her voice. "Why do you do that?" he asked as he thought of a way to soothe her.

"What do I do?"

He tossed words at her that she'd said to him at the cabin. "You answer with questions."

"You really don't play fair."

He watched her struggle not to smile. "Sure I do."

"I'm not sure I like it," she admitted about the apartment, because truth was such a part of their relationship. That elegant penthouse apartment with its priceless collections of paintings and statues had been so immaculate—sleek—as if whoever lived there swept through the rooms like a ghost that touched nothing. *No ghost lives there. You do.* Was Gillian Somerset as cold and unwelcoming as the place she called home? Ann met his stare. "Don't you think that's strange? It's my apartment. I chose the decor, so why don't I like it?"

She sat in the soft glow of morning sunlight. Without doing a thing, she made him yearn, ache. Too easily he could imagine more moments like this. "Your vision is blurred."

A sad, ironic smile curved her lips. "By amnesia? Do you think it's likely a person changes because of a bump on the head?"

As she bent her head, he reached out to stroke her cheek. "You won't know until you talk to family."

"Family?" She pressed her cheek against his warm, strong hand.

The simple vulnerable gesture nearly undid him.

"Is there family?" she asked, not for the first time.

Nick thought there might be many. The Somersets were well-known, though who they were in relation to her remained an unknown. "Parents, siblings, cousins—they exist."

But no one who'd missed her. There it was again. The painful reality she didn't want to face now that she knew her name. Pushing to a stand, she aired the anger that had as firm a grip on her as the confusion. "So what do I do? Do I go to the Somersets' door?" She whipped around and faced him. Too many walls were closing in on her. "What do I say to them? I don't know you, but do you know me? Tell me about myself?"

Despite all the emotional upheaval she'd gone through, Nick had never heard such strain in her voice before. Lightly he touched her hair, smoothed it. Even if he tried to do more to comfort her, she would accept only so much from him.

With the trill of the phone behind him, Nick stepped back and, in a brisk move, he snatched up the phone. While he responded to Riley, he watched her plunge plates and her hands into the soapy dishwater. "Do you have an address?" A shoulder against the kitchen wall, he cradled the receiver between his jaw and shoulder and reached for a nearby pencil. "Got it. Thanks, Riley."

Her stomach clenching, Ann concentrated on wiping away batter stubbornly caked to the side of a mixing bowl. An address for whom? Was the call about her? She drew some calming breaths. Not everything is about you.

Nick set the receiver in its cradle. "I called Riley earlier and asked him to find out if there was an elderly woman in Gillian Som—in your life," he said to her back.

Gillian Somerset doesn't exist for me, either, Ann wanted to say.

Nick didn't miss the unsteadiness of her hands when she lifted the dried bowl and set it to nestle in others. "Her name is Felicia Somerset. Your grandmother."

A grandmother? Restless, she reached for dried plates and stretched toward a cabinet to put them away. She learned in that instant that when upset, she didn't want to talk, she didn't want to be with anyone. She wanted to withdraw with her own thoughts. Thoughts that were troubled now.

Weren't grandmothers white haired, soft-spoken and kind? Didn't they love grandchildren unconditionally? Was that fantasy? It must be, if not, why hadn't the woman been worried about her? "I don't understand." Pivoting away, she snatched the sponge from the sink. "If I'm her granddaughter, why didn't she file a report with the police, with missing persons?"

Nick had considered the same question. Why wasn't the woman concerned about her granddaughter's absence? As Ann pretended interest in wiping off the counter, he sensed she wanted more than assurances. She didn't need comfort; she needed answers, ones he had to help her get. "You stay here. I'll visit Felicia Somerset and see what I can find out."

Ann didn't argue. Was she being a coward? Whether she was or not, she couldn't get herself to tell him that she was going with him. Why should she seek out people who didn't care about her? She closed her eyes, stilling as she heard the door close behind him. What she'd face now was almost as frightening as being nameless.

The wealth had been a given since the day Gillian Somerset was born. Nick slowed his car and traveled through gates on a cobblestone driveway that led past snow-covered grounds to an impressive stone house, guarded by towering oaks and willows.

At the ornate door, he looked away from the stained glass window to what he assumed were chauffeur quarters. Beyond the house were the tennis courts and a hedge of bushes.

When the door opened, Nick identified himself to an austere-looking butler. Minutes passed of Nick cooling his heels in the high-ceilinged entrance with its marbled floor and an antique-looking bench with spindly legs that appeared to be a perch for a more delicate bottom than his. He remained standing.

Easily seen was a winding stairway, chandeliers and, through French doors, a view of the lake.

"Mrs. Somerset will see you in the library," the butler announced from several feet away.

Nick followed, gathering impressions of old expensive furniture, though he knew zilch about antiques. Without a word, the butler opened the double doors to a library with walls of shelves containing leather-bound books.

The elderly woman he'd seen in photographs at Ann's apartment sat in a wheelchair behind an ornate cherry desk. She appeared more stately in person, the royal matriarch. Her gray hair, tucked up in a sort of bun, shone beneath the sunlight streaming in from a floor-to-ceiling window. She held her head high, meeting Nick with a steely gaze. "I've been informed that you have information about my granddaughter." Despite her fragile appearance, with her cool greeting she made it clear she was no pushover. "Let me warn you, I don't succumb easily to innuendos and threats. So you may drop the charade about being a detective and tell me who you really are and what you want."

"I don't know what you think I'm doing." Nick reached for his wallet and flipped it open to offer her identification. "But I am a cop."

"I see."

As she was silent for a second, Nick could imagine the thoughts racing through her mind.

"Young man, why is a policeman seeing me about my granddaughter?"

Chapter Seven

"She thought I was on vacation in Bermuda?" Ann sat down, feeling as if she were on a rocking boat.

Instead of everything making sense, Nick had left Felicia Somerset's house with more questions. At first, he'd thought there might be a chance Ann wasn't the woman's granddaughter. Then he'd seen Ann's photograph on a highly polished mahogany table. He'd assumed the grandmother had been led to believe her granddaughter had been basking in sunlight when she'd actually been caught in a Wisconsin storm. He'd followed gut instinct that he could trust her. If Ann had felt threatened by someone, it wasn't the grandmother.

"Bermuda?" Had she missed her plane and started to drive home but got lost? That made no sense. "Was I going alone?"

Nick didn't miss the distress that laced her voice heavily. "You called Felicia Somerset and said you were going there with Sara. The spur-of-the-moment trip surprised her."

Ann sighed in disgust at herself. "Who's Sara?"

"Sara Vandermein." The anguish in her eyes was startling similar to the expression Nick had seen in Felicia Somerset's. "A childhood friend."

Another person who should mean something to her was just a name, nothing more. She'd hoped this would be easier. "That's why she wasn't looking for me?"

Nick joined her on the sofa. "She'd assumed you were there. Although she admitted she was anxious that you didn't call. Usually when you were away, you maintained contact with her."

Oh, I want to stop this. I want to forget everything, Ann agonized. Everything he was telling her baffled her more. On a heavy sigh, she leaned into the strong shoulder so close to her. "Why was I going there?"

That seemed obvious to him. "For enjoyment." As her face turned up to him, Nick toyed with a strand of her hair.

Curiosity leading her now, Ann wondered about the woman he'd spoken to. "What is she like? My—my grandmother?"

Nick recalled the panic that had colored the woman's voice after he'd made his explanation about Ann's amnesia. "She had doubts at first about what I was telling her. I told her we ran a trace through the Motor Vehicle Department. That you've been to your apartment. She's concerned. She wanted to know if you were hurt. She wanted you to see a doctor, a specialist.'' He'd recalled wondering how to tell the woman that no amount of money would fix this problem. ''I told her the doctor said there isn't anything they can do. That you need time.''

Ann laid her head back on his shoulder. *Time*. She was beginning to hate that word. ''What else did you tell her?''

''I told her that the doctor thought something else was keeping you from remembering. When I asked her if something traumatic had happened, she told me that would be difficult to answer. It seems you're very independent.'' Nick saw a smile touch her eyes. ''As if we didn't know that. Whenever you've had a problem, you'd tell her after you'd dealt with it.'' He hadn't been surprised by those words. But whatever Ann had had to face this time had really unnerved her.

''She wanted to know where you were. I told her that you were with me.'' While genuine gratitude had come through clearly with the woman's thank-you, he'd nearly lost it when she'd told him that he'd be compensated for any expenses incurred. He'd taken a few long, even breaths, aware the temper that had flared had been from a memory past, not because of Felicia Somerset. It was Julia's parents who had tossed around money as if it were all-powerful and could make everything right in the world.

Ann remained silent as if considering his words. ''Is that all?''

''Pretty much.'' For a second, he weighed what else he'd learned, but only a second. From the beginning, Ann had counted on his honestly. "She said you're slow to trust people."

Hadn't she guessed that about herself? Yet except for the first night with Nick, she had trusted him.

"You allow only a few people to get close to you."

"I thought you'd go and—and I'd know the reason for everything." Facing him, she attempted to smile. "That hasn't happened."

The rest of her grandmother's words came back to him. Whenever Gillian was frightened, she would smile and pretend. Was the woman he knew that complex? He'd seen strength. But her grandmother had used the word *pretend.* He'd known another woman who'd been good at pretending, so much so he'd fallen in love and married her.

Ann's brows furrowed with a frown. "You told me what she said, but what is she like?"

"Velvet beneath steel."

With his description, Ann warmed to the woman even though they hadn't met. "You liked her?"

"I liked her," Nick said honestly. A weariness existed in her eyes that he hadn't seen before. He lifted the hand resting on her thigh and pressed his lips to her palm. "She wants to see you, Ann."

She stood, turning from him to stare out the window, and watched a crescent moon slip behind a cloud. "Do I still have choices?"

Nick bridged the distance to her and caressed a strand of her hair, then slid his fingers into others. Soft, sweet smelling, the silky strands fell around his fingers, luring him to her.

"I don't know if I want to go."

Nick crowded her, forcing her to turn in his arms. Though a familiar stubborn line creased her forehead, youthful uncertainty paled the color of her eyes. For a long moment, he simply held her. Touches were light, a stroke of a finger on her arm, a caress on his cheek. Raising his hands to her face, with his thumbs, he smoothed back her hair. "You want to see her," he said softly.

What she wanted was to forget everything—if just for one night. "I'm tired," Ann murmured. "Tired of analyzing everything. Who I am. Why I did something. What I feel." She placed a hand on his chest to feel the heat of him. Like all things in her life, she had questions about her emotions for him, too. But those she knew she could find answers for. "Especially what I feel with you." With a fingertip, Ann traced the outline of his lips. "When I'm here, when I'm with you—"

"Don't," he said quietly, to stop words she shouldn't say, words he wanted to hear. Obviously her emotions were running high; she was filled with doubts about who she was. Admirable thoughts, difficult ones, for he felt no uncertainty in the slim arm coiling around his neck, in the mouth that warmed his suddenly.

Ann closed her eyes. She craved time when her mind couldn't think, when all that mattered were feelings. Longing for him rushed her to take whatever they'd find, now, before the rest of the world swarmed in on them. Beneath her other hand on his chest, she felt his heart beating at the same quickened pace as her own. "I want to make new memories," she said between uneven breaths.

Nick inhaled harshly, stunned that he had to grapple with control. He knew her vulnerability and his own. "I won't stop." He wouldn't be able to.

His eyes swept over her face as if trying to see inside her mind. All she wanted was to hold on to what she had found. Because of him, she'd discovered feelings even when she hadn't known if she would ever learn anything else about herself. Because of him, a new world had opened to her. She didn't want to let any part of it go. "I don't want you to stop," she whispered against his mouth.

With a desperation that he thought would unman him, Nick pulled her closer. Tomorrow might end what had barely had time to start. But that was tomorrow. Tonight, now, he filled himself with the sweetness of her taste. He wanted to give her tenderness, but a need that promised to push him over the edge possessed him. With her mouth slanting across his, he trailed his fingers along her thigh and he cupped the softness of her breast. He knew he'd never tell her that every anxious moment she'd had he'd felt. He could only offer himself. There could be no promises between them. She had to know that. All he could give her was now, a little time to forget.

He wished for patience; he possessed none. Hungry, his lips twisted across hers, answering the play of her mouth, the sweet and savoring play. Urgent, his hands moved more demandingly over her. He'd been her protector, her friend. Now, as desire licked at him, he ached to be her lover. He gathered her hair in his hand, kissing her hard. It wasn't enough. He knew it wouldn't be. She filled his mind. There would be a price to pay. As a cop he'd learned that, but for these moments, he'd willingly face it, whatever it was.

On a soft moan, Ann went with the rightness of the moment. For her, this was real. Nothing else. Kisses blended. Hot, thorough kisses. Eyes closed, she lost herself to him, to the hands lifting her sweater from her and cupping her breast, to the roughness of his chin across her collarbone, to her skin tingling beneath his every touch and each heated caress of his mouth. She knew she was in his arms, clinging as they journeyed through the cool dark house. Then she felt herself floating to the bed. To have more awareness of anything meant thinking.

She couldn't think. She pulled him to her, sinking him against her. She helped him shrug out of his shirt, tugged at the buckle of his belt, at denim, shoving it from his hips. The coolness in the room caressed her breasts as his mouth lingered at the edge of lace on her bra, as he pushed the wispy silk away. Then pleasure swarmed in on her. He kissed first one breast, then the other, catching a nipple, stroking it with his tongue. As he fed on her, like a blind person, she splayed her fingers, letting them roam down the flat ripples of his chest. Her hands as eager and greedy as his, she reveled in the sleekness of his flesh, the bunching muscles of his back. He felt strong and warm. He felt wonderful.

Lost in him, she gave. As she tore breath from him, he made her gasp to keep pace with the madness. Soft and yielding, weak, she closed her eyes again as strong, callused hands taunting her blazed a trail to her belly and lower.

Sounds, soft and urgent, slipped from her lips with each moist stroke of his tongue gliding across her body. She arched to meet the heat of his mouth, the caress of his tongue. He murmured something unintelligible. Words didn't matter.

Through a cloud of desire, she heard his raspy breaths blending with hers. A burning need engulfed her. She needed. Simply needed. When he shifted, she clutched his arms and wrapped her legs around him. And she felt a control in her life that she'd begun to hunger for.

Head back, she opened her eyes to the face above hers. Breathless, her skin damp with passion, she whispered his name and raised her hips to him. As flesh met flesh, she gripped him to her, welcoming his heat and hardness, not wondering if she'd ever felt like this before. She took him into her body, absorbing the warmth and fullness of him. There was no before. There was only now—and this man.

How much time had passed seemed unimportant. As they remained tangled together, hearts still beating hard against each other, Ann released a long sigh of contentment and continued to cling to him. Though she might not understand herself, her feelings for him seemed crystal clear. She wanted more time like this, listening to his breaths, feeling the beat of his heart. With so much wrong in her life, it amazed her that she felt so happy.

Not wanting to lose the dreamy aftermath of loving, she skimmed a finger along his side, down the lean, muscular flesh that she'd touched and tasted. There had been another before him. She spoke her thought. "I wasn't a virgin." Whenever she'd lost her innocence seemed unimportant. But she couldn't imagine she'd known the same heat, the same aching, the same yearning to feel as one with any other man.

Shifting, Nick rolled to his back and cradled her against him. Beneath the shadowy mantle of night, he stared at the dark ceiling and idly sifted his fingers through her hair to find the sensitive spot near her earlobe. What she'd said didn't matter to him. Now was all he cared about. "Neither was I," he murmured to keep her from thinking he'd expected her to be.

"Were there many?"

He felt as if he'd never been with another. "One I thought mattered, and didn't." And one that does, and shouldn't. He doubted the staying power of what they'd found, but once wasn't enough, wouldn't be. "You were all I could want." Against him, he felt her catch her breath as he stroked her inner thigh.

Bending his head, he sought the taste that he craved as intensely as an addiction. With a kiss, one kiss, he knew sanity would slip away again. And nothing would curb what had begun. Nothing, he acknowledged when she pulled away to brace herself over him.

He managed to draw one quick breath when her head lowered and her tongue roamed lazily over his belly. With tender caresses and feather-light kisses, she flirted with his control. Then her magic snatched all thoughts from him.

A sky, gray with predawn light, greeted Nick when he stepped outside and began running. As the cold morning air filled his lungs, he faced one problem. He wanted to think of a future, of tomorrows with her. The night and excitement stole good sense. He couldn't follow those feelings. A life was unfolding for her. Until she knew what it was, he had no business thinking about anything except the day-to-day with her.

For blocks he ran hard, until winded. As he reached the porch steps, he drew a few long, deep breaths. His face burning from the cold that promised more snow, he entered the kitchen, then flopped onto a kitchen chair. He'd pushed himself, hoping a little physical pain would snap him back to reality. It had: he knew now he was falling in love with her.

In the bedroom, shafts of dim morning sunlight pierced through the blinds into the room. Awake, alone, Ann stretched then lazily she shoved the blanket aside. She forced herself from the bed and dressed quickly. She could disregard the soft caresses, the hot kisses and still feel the same about him. When with him, a downpour of emotion rushed through her. He calmed and comforted. He offered strength when she needed it, and he allowed her to find her own when sympathy would weaken her. She was in love with him. Or falling in love with him. She wasn't quite sure which, but she clung to the mood making her smile when she breezed into the kitchen.

"I was going to let you sleep longer."

Startled, she whirled around. Slouched on a chair at the kitchen table, Nick sat in shadow. "You were sitting in the dark?"

Before the world she needed to rediscover crashed down on them, they had time. "I stopped being afraid of the dark at four," he said, grinning wryly to keep the smile on her face.

"Were you one of those tough kids?"

"Swaggered." From outside, a familiar meow cut into the silence.

A laugh bubbled in Ann's throat because he looked torn between disbelief and amusement. She gave him her best I'm-innocent look. Of course, she wasn't. She and the cat were becoming buddies.

"That cat's going to think he belongs here," he grumbled, rising from the chair. While she poured coffee, he bent his head to kiss her neck. The scent of her, clean and fresh and womanly, was a part of him now. Lightly he ran taunting kisses along her jaw, grazing skin so soft and warm that just by touching it, the feverish rush of last night seemed only a breath away.

Smiling, Ann angled her head to the side to give him more freedom. "Is *that cat* his name?"

"Forget that cat," he murmured, sensuously tracing the cord in her neck. "Why do you always taste so wonderful?"

She laughed, a sultry sound that slithered over him. "You must be very hungry."

Food wasn't on his mind. Nothing was—except her. He wanted this time with her. He wanted every damn moment he could have. He wanted to forget everything that had happened yesterday, and he couldn't.

"You're looking too serious," Ann teased when he suddenly stepped away. Actually, brooding. Don't regret everything now, she wanted to beg. How could she explain to anyone, even him, that what he'd given her was more than she'd hoped for?

"You're dodging what's inevitable," Nick said, unable to look at her and force this moment.

He'd be her conscience, just as he'd been her friend, Ann realized. "I want one more day."

As she came up behind him, he couldn't resist the craving to feel her in his arms again. Turning, he gathered her close. "Before what happens? What are you worried about?"

She spoke of the uneasiness rustling inside her whenever she dropped her guard. "Before I don't have choices anymore."

Nick kissed the tip of her nose. "I was wrong about that." He brushed his lips across her eyebrow. "You're too much your own person not to have them. You'll always have them," he said, before lowering his head and kissing her.

In silence, Ann sat beside him in the car during the trip to Felicia Somerset's estate. She noted he cruised Lake Shore Drive northward, past the city, and detoured to let her absorb the snow-covered landscapes of the suburbs. Serene as the drive was past woods and stately estates, Ann grew tenser as she studied each one. "Am I supposed to recognize something here?"

His heart went out to her, not with pity, but with a need to shoulder some of the agony he sensed within her. "Not necessarily." Nick pulled onto what used to be a country road before the suburbs closed in on it and weaved a route through one affluent suburb that he knew well. He negotiated a turn past a prestigious English manor house that he'd foolishly called home five years ago.

Not ten minutes from it, he drove the final turn toward the lakefront and old mansions, then passed the double wrought-iron gates onto the long driveway of the Somerset estate.

Ann hunched forward, placing her hands on the dashboard, and peered at the palatial house. It offered no flash of recognition, no revelation. It looked like a castle. Did she have mean stepsisters? She stifled a laugh, certain her life had been no fairy tale. Princesses didn't run away from their castles.

Though fighting for courage, she didn't hesitate when Nick flicked off the ignition. She stepped from the car and stood on legs that suddenly seemed to weigh a ton.

"It's going to be okay." Nick cupped her elbow. "There's a lady who loves you inside that house."

The weight of her own doubts bore down on her. "Does she?"

"Yes," he said with so much certainty she accepted his opinion as truth. But then from the beginning, she'd believed what he'd said to her.

Because she knew he was looking for a smile, she

managed a strained one, but the tension coiled around her like a tight spring when they were ushered into the elegant hallway. Afraid to think, she concentrated on the sound of the butler's footsteps echoing through rooms. A distinguished man with snow-white hair and clear blue eyes, he'd been polite and had looked almost relieved to see her. Was he merely an employee or someone who'd become an extended part of the family?

Too anxious, she paced, catching her reflection in a gilt-edged mirror. Could that woman have lived here? Had she really spent her childhood in such a dignified atmosphere? The silence surrounding her was unnerving, the only sound coming from a grandfather clock at the end of the hallway. Visually she coursed a path up the curving staircase, one already familiar from her dream.

At the pressure of Nick's hand on the small of her back, Ann noticed the butler had reappeared. His posture erect, he led them down a hallway, past what appeared to be a ballroom, then to what Ann assumed was a drawing room.

"Gillian." The woman sitting in the wheelchair was, as Nick had described her during the drive, small and frail-looking but elegant. "Sit near, dear," she requested.

It was the slight tremble as she spoke that propelled Ann forward into the room of muted grays and blues and silk-upholstered sofas and chairs. *I don't know you. I wish I did.* When the woman extended her hand, Ann hesitated. Pain flashed in the woman's pale eyes. This has to be as hard on someone who cares about me as it is for me, Ann reflected.

Not wanting to hurt anyone, she stretched out her arm until her fingers met the woman's. A hand as soft as velvet touched hers and urged her to a chair within arm's length. Though it felt strange, Ann kept her hand in the woman's and stared hard at her face.

"You don't recognize me?" she asked.

"No, I'm sorry. I don't."

Something close to grief pulled down the woman's features, but her wrinkled hand patted Ann's while she offered encouraging words. "Don't worry."

How easily everyone said that to her, Ann mused. With difficulty, she drew a breath to overcome a tightening in her chest. Was it the start of an anxiety attack? She thought it might be, because she wanted to flee, escape all the unknowns. She peered at Nick. When she'd first entered the room, he'd taken a position near the fireplace. Lounging against the mantel, he swept a slow, appraising look around the room.

"I'm sure the detective told you," Felicia said, recapturing Ann's attention. "I had no idea that you weren't in Bermuda. If I—" She paused, pressing her lips together.

"I'm really all right." Ann strived to sound calm, suddenly aware of the distress in the woman's face. "Except I have no personal memory." Were there others she would have to offer a similar explanation to? "My parents. Are they here?"

Her grandmother's brow wrinkled. "My dear, your father died when you were twelve. Your mother's been gone several years."

NO COST! NO OBLIGATION TO BUY!
NO PURCHASE NECESSARY!

PLAY "LUCKY 7"
AND GET AS MANY AS FIVE FREE GIFTS...

HOW TO PLAY:

1 With a coin, carefully scratch away the gold panel opposite. Then check the claim chart to see what we have for you – FREE BOOKS and gift – ALL YOURS! ALL FREE!

2 Send back this card and you'll receive specially selected Silhouette Special Edition® novels. These books are yours to keep absolutely FREE.

3 There's no catch. You're under no obligation to buy anything. We charge nothing for your first shipment. And you don't have to make any minimum number of purchases – not even one!

4 The fact is thousands of readers enjoy receiving books by mail from the Reader Service™. They like the convenience of home delivery and they like getting the best new romance novels at least a month before they are available in the shops. And of course postage and packing is completely FREE!

5 We hope that after receiving your free books you'll want to remain a subscriber. But the choice is yours – to continue or cancel, any time at all! So why not take up our invitation, with no risk of any kind. You'll be glad you did!

You'll look like a million dollars when you wear this lovely necklace! Its cobra-link chain is a generous 18" long, and the beautiful puffed heart pendant will add the finishing touch to any outfit!

Play

"Lucky 7"

E8AI

Just scratch away the gold panel with a coin.
Then check below to see how many FREE GIFTS will be yours.

YES! I have scratched away the gold panel. Please send me all the gifts for which I qualify. I understand that I am under no obligation to purchase any books, as explained on the opposite page. I am over 18 years of age.

BLOCK CAPITALS PLEASE

MS/MRS/MISS/MR
_____

ADDRESS
_____

_____

POSTCODE
_____

▶ DETACH AND POST CARD TODAY ▶

WORTH FOUR FREE BOOKS
PLUS A PUFFED HEART NECKLACE

WORTH FOUR FREE BOOKS

WORTH THREE FREE BOOKS

WORTH TWO FREE BOOKS

The Reader Service™

FREEPOST
Croydon
Surrey
CR9 3WZ

NO
STAMP
NEEDED

If offer card is missing, write to: The Reader Service, P.O. Box 236, Croydon, Surrey CR9 3RU.

No parents. She felt nothing. Did they love her? Did they have wonderful moments together? She grieved, not for them but for what she couldn't remember. "So I lived with her, then you?"

Felicia averted her watchful gaze. "Perhaps we should discuss this later."

Nick caught her quick, apprehensive glance his way. Without knowing why, he couldn't rescue her.

Ann released an impatient sigh. "I want to know."

"Your mother was sickly. So you and she lived with me since you were ten."

She's shielding me from something. Would she, if she didn't care for me? "I should thank you then."

"For what?" Felicia asked on a tremulous breath. "Loving you?"

Because of the unshed tears glazing her grandmother's eyes, Ann attempted a weak smile. "That's good to know."

In a tentative manner, Felicia leaned forward and placed a hand lightly on her cheek. "Never doubt that."

Someone really did love her. She wanted to cry because she'd found that person and felt nothing for her. She didn't want to distress this woman, but she needed to know everything. "I realize you might try to spare me from what might be sad memories, but I really don't have any. So anything you say doesn't carry any emotion with it."

"I understand." The sorrow in her grandmother's voice forced Ann to accept that unwittingly she'd probably hurt her often. "You always were adamant about truth, no matter how painful it might be." Her grandmother met her with sad eyes. "Your parents were divorced before your father died."

Translated, that meant what? Her childhood hadn't been happy? "So I didn't see him often?"

"No, you didn't."

Why not? Because her mother wouldn't let her? This woman was her father's mother, yet she'd allowed her daughter-in-law and granddaughter to live with her. Had she turned her back on her son? Why would she? "I don't have any brothers or sisters, do I?" she asked.

"No, you were an only child."

Disappointment coursed through Ann. She supposed she'd hoped for the closeness she'd witnessed between Nick and his sisters. She shook the thought away. What she needed to be concerned with was the part of her past her mind refused to remember. And her future. "What do I do?"

"Do, my dear?" Her grandmother looked puzzled.

"Do I work?"

Felicia's shoulders relaxed as if a weight had been lifted from them, as if she considered the worst questions over with. "You have no need."

Ann wondered how that was possible. Being busy, washing dishes, cleaning house at Nick's had kept her sanity intact during days of limbo. "Then what do I do?"

"You love to ride. We have a stable, and—" Felicia paused, her thin lips spreading into a more relaxed smile. "You've always enjoyed shopping and traveling. And you are quite involved in charities.

You also are an excellent actress. You've appeared in several Junior League fund-raising plays.''

Playing catch-up with her own life in minutes seemed impossible, yet Ann tried. When her nerves roused again, she took a moment to compose herself before asking a question that seemed more important than any other suddenly. Briefly she glanced at Nick, then directed her attention back to her grandmother. ''I have an apartment of my own. So I'm not married, am I?'' she blurted.

''This must be so difficult for you.'' Compassion filled her grandmother's tone. ''No, you aren't married.''

More than relief washed over her. Since a night of loving with Nick, she'd agonized about another man existing who might expect her love.

''Aunt Felicia,'' a voice called out from the doorway. A small blonde about the same age as Ann, with an amazingly deep tan for November, glided into the room. ''Gillian.'' Her voice sang with the greeting. ''I didn't know you were back.'' She let the last word die, her eyes darting to Nick. ''Well, hello.''

''Stephanie, this is Nicholas Vincetti,'' Felicia announced. ''My niece Stephanie,'' she said, finishing the introduction.

Nick nodded and watched Ann closely. A faint line of concentration cut its way between her brows. Was she mulling over the name? Was this too hard on her? What would have thrown a strong woman so badly that she would want to forget it?

''You didn't get a tan, Gillian.'' Her cousin arched

a brow and sent a speculative glance at Nick. "What were you doing in Bermuda?"

"Stephanie," Felicia interrupted, "sit for a moment." She proceeded to explain about Ann's memory loss.

"Amnesia?" Her cousin wrinkled her nose. "You have amnesia? Oh, Gillian, how awful that must be." Curiosity slipped into her expression. "Are you saying you don't even—"

"Now, Stephanie, that's enough," Felicia said sternly.

"But how frightening that must be."

Was she close to this woman? Ann wondered. "I am getting tired." With the lie out, she swung an appealing look at Nick. She didn't want to answer questions, she wanted to ask them.

"Of course. We can talk more tomorrow," Felicia assured her. "Do you want to stay here tonight instead of at your apartment?"

Ann preferred Nick's home. She kept the thought to herself. "No, I'll leave, but I'll be back." It took effort to make that promise. She didn't want to upset her grandmother, but she wished for one thing. To hide in Nick's house and not leave it again until she awakened from this nightmare.

"As soon as you're feeling better, we can go shopping," Stephanie piped in. "That will make you feel better. It always did. We'll fly to Paris, like we always do, and—"

"Stephanie," Felicia said again, with more demand in her tone. "She needs rest."

Her cousin's eyes widened with alarm. "You're not well?"

Ann thought the question odd. Physically she felt wonderful. True, she still had a nagging ache occasionally in her head, mostly when she tried to remember too much. But all that seemed wrong with her was that she lacked her past. The look in her cousin's eyes carried a message of something more dire. Did Stephanie view amnesia as a mental illness? "Just tired," Ann said again.

That answer seemed to satisfy her cousin. "You'll be fine," she said, almost airily. "Redmond will be glad you're back. He's been moping around the club."

Standing with Nick near the arched doorway now, Ann felt her stomach roll. There was someone else she had to feel guilty about, someone else she couldn't remember. "Who's Redmond?"

Stephanie stared at her as if she'd grown two heads. "Your fiancé."

Fiancé. Stunned, Ann sat in the car beside Nick, still reeling from the news that she was to wed some man named Redmond Harper at the beginning of next month.

"An old family friend," her grandmother had told her.

"The wedding had been planned for later, but you moved it forward," her cousin had informed her. "With the rush, you and Redmond decided to make it a smaller wedding and invite only five hundred close friends."

With that ludicrous remark, Ann had had to stifle a nervous laugh. No one had that many close friends. Was everything in the world she'd come from so superficial? "This doesn't make sense to me," Ann said, finally breaking the silence between her and Nick when he zipped his car into the underground parking garage of her high-rise. "Women who are happily engaged don't get in a car and drive hundreds of miles away," she said in a frustrated, angry tone. When he opened the door for her, she glanced up, but he said nothing. In fact, he'd been quiet ever since they'd left her grandmother's home. "I'd like to walk."

As she stepped away, Nick slammed the car door. He had no part in her life, except to help her get back her past. During the drive, he'd dealt with the bombshell that some other man had won her heart. Now it was time for him to stop acting like a fool. So he was falling in love with her. No, with a woman named Ann, he reminded himself. Gillian Somerset had a future with another man. And what he felt didn't matter. What was important was why she'd been on that road that rainy night. And what had happened between her and a friend named Sara.

"Stephanie said she'd call me later and give me Sara's phone number," Ann said when he was beside her.

As her shoulder brushed his, Nick nearly put an arm around her. He had no rights. Another man existed. She might not remember him yet, but she would. "You need to talk to her, and find out why you didn't go to Bermuda as you planned."

The winter chill sweeping through her, she huddled deeper in her coat. ''Nick, I have never heard of anyone named Sara. I don't remember anyone by that name.'' Or a man named Redmond.

At the crosswalk, Nick caught her arm as a car approached. Snow flurries danced on the beams of the headlights. ''You must have a personal phone book in your apartment. Let's go there and get it instead of waiting for your cousin's phone call.'' He thought that sounded like a wise action. Unlike his home, in her apartment, he'd be more likely to remember that she belonged to a different world.

Chapter Eight

"Okay, you look in the bedroom," Nick said when they entered her apartment. A twist of the lock on the door, a kiss, he thought, and they'd both drift free of all that seemed to be closing around them—separating them. What good would that do? Reality would rush back at them. Nothing would be different. "I'll check the desk in the living room."

Ann ached to stop him from moving away. She'd thought she'd seen a warm, wanting look in his eyes. At that moment, she'd wanted to plead with him. Hold me, kiss me, make me forget. She'd remained silent, knowing he wouldn't touch her. Honorable, scrupulous, he'd remind her of a fiancé she didn't even know.

Inside the bedroom, she began a hunt for some kind of personal phone book. A cousin Stephanie, a friend named Sara. Neither of them meant anything to her. Worse was the knowledge that some man, a man she couldn't even visualize, expected her to marry him. Her stomach somersaulted as she bent over a dresser drawer. Stephanie had said his name was Redmond. Was he the man in the photographs she and Nick had found? Blond, clean-cut, lanky, he looked like someone who played tennis a lot, someone used to a leisurely life-style. Did that mean she was, too?

Hearing Nick rummaging through a drawer in the other room, she knuckled down to the task at hand and searched dresser drawers. In the bottom one, she found a small white box containing a cameo locket. It looked old and expensive. Was it from Felicia? Her grandmother, she reminded herself. She'd seen pain in the woman's eyes when she entered Felicia's home. Compassion had nudged Ann to hug the woman, but how could she? She didn't know her, either.

Closing the drawer, she pushed to her feet. In the living room, Nick was perched on the white hassock, bending forward with a book in his hands. "You found it?"

With his nod, she stepped close and took the book from him. It was opened to a page with Redmond Harper's name on it. Swiftly she turned the page, then thumbed through others until she found the phone number and address for Sara Vandermein. "Should I call her first? It seems wrong to burst in on the woman." As deadly serious eyes met hers, the excuse fell lame. He didn't need to say a word. She read his thought. She was being a coward to avoid another stranger, another explanation.

Peripherally she caught Nick's movement. That's when she heard the chime of the doorbell. As Nick started toward the door, she stepped into his path and placed a hand on his arm. "No." Weary from the moments with her grandmother and cousin, she toyed with the idea of not answering. All she wanted now was to go back to Nick's house. But since any visitors needed clearance from the doorman, she speculated that her late-night guest wasn't a stranger to Gillian Somerset, just to her. "I'll answer it."

"Ann." With a fingertip, Nick touched her chin. Her eyes appeared larger, shadowed with an exhaustion that her body didn't reveal.

Ann offered him a strained smile. "Word traveled fast that I've returned."

Nick had had the same thought. "I'll open the door," he said, still uncertain that she hadn't felt threatened by someone.

She let a protest die. Would she recognize the person on the other side of the door? Her mind crowded with the faces of her apartment building's doorman, her grandmother, the butler, her cousin. And smiling ones in dozens of photographs. Why didn't even one of them look familiar? Disturbed, she stood beside Nick and frowned as he opened the door. Immediately she was swept into masculine arms.

"Darling."

Pure willpower kept Ann from jerking free of an embrace. This was the fiancé. She recognized him, though his blond hair had been cut shorter, his tan appeared deeper, and he looked shorter and thinner than he had in the photographs.

"I've heard. My poor darling." Drawing back, with his hands possessively tight on her shoulders, he inclined his head to greet her with a kiss.

Ann turned her face from him, and over his shoulder, she caught Nick's squint in their direction. The kiss landed on her cheek, but the man holding her seemed unfazed, making her wonder if he was content with little pecks of affection. She knew another man who demanded much more.

"Redmond Harper?" Nick let the door remain open. "That is who you are, isn't it?" He'd assessed the man quickly as moneyed, well-bred and haughty.

Sharp and arrogant eyes slashed to Nick. "And who are you?"

Before the situation got out of hand, Ann eased from Redmond's embrace and took control, introducing Nick.

"Oh, the policeman who brought you back here," Redmond interjected before Ann could say more. "How fortunate that our men in blue do occasionally come through at appropriate times," he quipped with a look back at her.

Only Ann noticed Nick narrowing his eyes dangerously.

"I've been beside myself worrying about you, Gillian." Not as unaware of Nick as he'd like to pretend, he cast another quick look at him while he maneuvered Ann to the living room. Ann stiffened as his hand gripped hers. He must have felt it. A laugh that sounded humorless edged his words. "Surely, you don't mean that you don't remember me?"

Everyone kept saying something similar to her. Exhausted, she wanted silence, just a few minutes of silence. "I don't remember leaving here."

He faced her with a frown. It lasted only a second. "That would explain everything then. When your grandmother told me you'd left with Sara for Bermuda, I was quite peeved that you'd gone without telling me, without even a goodbye, especially with our wedding only weeks away."

Why would she do that to the man she loved? Ann wondered. Was she so inconsiderate? He kept staring at her now with expectation. Was he anticipating an apology? How could she mouth one without knowing if he deserved it?

"Now, I'm told that you didn't go on that trip with Sara."

Ann looked past him to Nick. He'd moved to inside the doorway and now stood with his shoulder braced against the wall. Nerves tightening, she wondered how to get rid of the man touching her again so she could stop questions she couldn't answer. "I was wandering in the woods and walked up to Nick's cabin."

"Why were you there?" One question flowed into another as his long, narrow fingers closed over her left hand. "Where is your ring? Did you lose it?"

Ann looked down. So there had been one. Again she stared at Nick. How different her feelings had been for him when she'd contemplated the same question in the cabin?

"Officer." Tightly, and in a proprietary manner, Redmond kept Ann's hand clutched in his. "Thank you. I'll stay with my fiancée now. You may leave."

A corner of Nick's mouth curved in a grin at the man's tone of dismissal. "Can't do that."

Ann didn't miss the dangerous glint in Nick's eyes.

"You can't—" Redmond turned a puzzled look on Ann. "Why are the police even involved?"

Ann shrugged. "I suppose because of my amnesia." Eager for the quiet of the kitchen, she stepped toward it. "Would you like coffee, Redmond?" she asked quickly. No way did she feel up to dealing with a jealous fiancé.

"Coffee? But Gillian. Ramona isn't here, is she?"

Ann froze in midstride and swung a look over her shoulder at him. God, not someone else. "Ramona?"

Sympathy oozed from him. "How terrible this is for you. You don't remember your maid."

"Maid? Ramona is my maid?"

"And your cook." He moved toward her. "Sweetheart, I doubt if you even know where the coffeepot is."

Ann backed up a few steps to keep distance between them.

"How did you know the maid wasn't here?" Nick asked.

"I assumed she wasn't, since she didn't open the door," Redmond said to Ann as if she'd asked the question. "Weeks ago, you gave her time off to take a trip and visit relatives." Looking down, he tugged on the white starched cuff of his shirt. "About this

Bermuda jaunt you told your grandmother you were taking.''

Shaking her head, Ann rushed words. ''I don't remember making plans for it or what happened that I didn't.''

''Hush. Don't get excited,'' he said softly in the manner of someone speaking to a small, confused child. ''You'll be fine in a few days, darling,'' he added as if he'd spoken a fact.

''Yes. I just need rest,'' she said, and skirted around him toward the door.

''If you're sure you'll be—''

''I'll be fine,'' Ann interrupted with a backward glance, glad to see he was only steps behind her.

''I'll call tomorrow, darling.''

Ann turned her cheek to receive another peck of a kiss. ''Fine,'' she said with a weak smile. She kept it plastered on her face until he stepped into the hall.

As Nick shut the door, she released a groan and sagged against him. Who was the woman her grandmother had declared had never worked? The one her cousin had insisted loved to shop and travel? She'd sounded so shallow. She had to be someone else. This all had to be a mistake. She couldn't be Gillian Somerset. She couldn't be that woman. She didn't remember her grandmother or a man she was supposed to marry. ''I felt nothing for him, Nick.'' Even Redmond's touch had bothered her. She wasn't being fair to him, she knew. Of course, she'd feel uncomfortable with him. He was a stranger to her. But another man had found a place in her heart. ''What did you think of him?''

A loaded question, Nick mused. "I'm not the person to ask."

She understood the meaning behind his words, but his opinion mattered to her.

With her face against his, something deeper, more intense than the love Nick felt for her swarmed in on him. He wanted to protect her from more pain, and he realized that quite possibly he might be the cause of it if he didn't back away. If he could do nothing else, he swore he wouldn't be the reason for more confusion, more hurt in her life.

On a shuddery breath, Ann raised her face to look at him. The cop stood before her, expressionless. Was he distancing himself? She couldn't let him, not now. As his hands moved to her shoulders, she shook her head to stop him from stepping away. "I need you," she said, holding on to him.

Nick's gut knotted. She'd never said those words to him before. Since he'd met her, she'd shown an indescribable resolve not to fall to pieces. "Ann, there's someone else," he said, even as he sensed how much those words cost her. She had to face reality. He had to.

"I don't know him." Didn't he understand that the turmoil in her life had nothing to do with them? "I don't remember him. How can I be unfaithful to someone who means nothing to me?"

"What about when you do?"

"Oh, Nick." She brought her lips close to his. She wanted to cry with the realization that she might lose far more than she was willing to give up. "Don't shut me out. I need you."

Fiercely he hugged her and felt the rhythm of her heart beating against him. A desire slipped over him to ask her to leave with him, to walk away from everything else. He couldn't ask that, and he couldn't turn away from her.

Winter arrived with gusto the next morning. Wind swept snow across the car window as Nick drove Ann to her friend's address. Every moment brought her closer to her past and farther away from him. But until he was certain she was happy with what she'd found, until she was certain it was what she wanted, he couldn't let her go. "Do you remember this?" he asked, when he was braking in the curving driveway of a massive white home.

Ann shot a look at the Georgian house. "No." She grabbed another steadying breath to meet someone she was supposed to know.

Instead of a maid, Sara Vandermein answered her own door. Sleek dark hair that swayed with her movement curtained a face with prominent cheekbones and an aristocratic nose. The woman greeted her with a hug that felt sincere. "I'm so glad you're home." Her dark gaze swept over Nick. Luxurious lashes framed her eyes, giving her a seductive look. "You're the policeman?"

Nick eyed her with a thoughtful expression. Who'd been the grapevine? The cousin Stephanie or the fiancé? "That's me." Deliberately he stayed at a distance. In a cozy twosome with Ann, her friend might prove more informative.

"Why don't the policemen who stop me for speeding ever look like that?" she said in a stage whisper to Ann, then with ease, she linked her arm with Ann's. "Come in and sit down."

She's as nervous as I am, Ann decided as Sara rambled about a spa she'd been to.

"You'd love it." Sara rolled her eyes. "I hated it, but then I'm happily lazy. And you never were." She perched on a pink-and-lavender brocade sofa across from a matching one Ann sat on. "I must admit that I don't know what to say to you. You don't remember me, do you?"

Ann wanted to warm to a woman who'd apparently been a longtime friend. "No, I don't."

Sara's lips curved in a slim smile. "Then I'll have to help you play catch-up, so you know who's disgusting, but first tell me everything."

Nearly an hour later, Ann was crossing the plush white carpet to leave. Seeing her friend's frown, she mustered a forced smile to lighten the moment. "Thank you." Did she often hide real feelings behind phony smiles? she wondered. From the corner of her eye, she saw Nick step outside. "I'm sorry I came without calling first."

In answer, Sara returned what sounded like a subdued snort. "You never called first." As Ann retrieved leather gloves from her pockets, Sara touched the tips of hair brushing Ann's shoulders. "I like it this way. You look good with it styled so straight."

So she'd worn it differently. "Thank you."

"Why don't we have lunch in a few days?" Sara brushed Ann's cheek with hers. "I'll call Stephanie and Trish. The four of us can sample one of the Bis-

tro's more decadent desserts. *Profiterolles au choco-
lat,* perhaps.''

Who was Trish? Another friend? ''Perhaps,'' Ann
responded before walking away from her and toward
the car.

As Ann settled in the car with Nick, she considered
her conversation with Sara. ''She seemed nice, but
I'm never sure how to respond to people,'' she admitted. ''I liked her but—'' She felt Nick glance her
way and knew she'd have to finish. ''I don't feel toward people the way they feel toward me. And that
makes me feel like such a phony.''

''You're trying to spare their feelings.''

''Yes, I know I am, but that doesn't keep me from
feeling deceitful,'' she said disgustedly. Her identity
still eluded her, but she was beginning to understand
herself. Truth mattered to her. ''And I learned nothing. I don't have any more idea why I told my grandmother that I was taking a trip, going to Bermuda
with Sara.''

''You know plenty. You know now that you never
planned a trip with her,'' he said, reminding her of
what Sara had said.

''But why did I lie? I don't understand. Why would
I phone my grandmother and say I was going somewhere with Sara if I wasn't?'' Ann drew an uneasy
breath. ''Was lying to my grandmother typical behavior? And what did she mean when she said that
Redmond sometimes exasperated me?''

Nick said nothing. Since the visit to her friend, was
she coming to grips with what he'd known from the

beginning? What was proper carried a lot of weight among some classes. "I thought she answered you."

Ann shifted on the car seat, discomforted by the meaning behind Sara's answer. "He's suitable."

"Makes sense."

Ann had been stunned, wondering if Sara was implying that she didn't love Redmond. Sara had assured her that she probably did, since there had been enough other men from their circle of friends, appropriate ones to choose from. How cold and unemotional that had sounded, Ann thought. Why would that be so important to her? Hadn't the woman she'd been cared about love? Impatience had surged through her. All she knew now was what Sara had offered as an explanation. When she was troubled, she took off. She always kept big problems to herself. "To me, nothing makes sense."

Ann repeated those words later that evening for a different reason. Though she and Nick had dinner and saw a movie, he'd left her at the door, not even kissing her goodbye.

In the morning, sidewalks and streets glistened with a layer of light frost. The chill and the promise of the cold wind on her face luring her outside, she was nearly to the door when the phone rang.

She spent the next ten minutes talking to her grandmother and sipping tea before she finally stepped outside.

Bundled in a fleece-lined parka that seemed more appropriate for ski slopes than city streets, she tucked leather-gloved hands into her pockets and ambled

from one street to the next. Even as her life became
more complicated, she was becoming more comfortable with it. Now she'd faced the people she didn't
know who loved her, an engagement with a man she
didn't want. She was nagged by guilt about Redmond.
How could she pretend she loved him?

And what about Nick? Since awakening, she'd fret-
ted about him, about them. The fault for her doubts
clearly rested on his shoulders. What else could she
believe? Even though he'd said he'd be by at eleven,
she sensed he was pulling away from her. How could
he? Just because she'd learned more about herself, her
feelings for him hadn't changed. Could she have
imagined his tenderness and concern? Could a man
make love as he had and feel nothing?

Shoving back the cuff of her parka, she checked
the gold watch she'd found in her jewelry box last
night. She had only a few minutes before Nick arrived. Nearing the door of her apartment building,
Ann smiled at the doorman, a tall, gray-haired man
with a heavily lined face. As he opened the door for
her, she saw Nick slouched against the wall beside
him. "You're early."

"Just got here."

She responded to his easy smile. Possibly she was
worrying about them unnecessarily.

"Do you remember Harry?" Nick asked, motioning with his head to the doorman.

Ann saw none of the previous guardedness in the
doorman's alert blue eyes.

"We've been talking," Nick said, touching the
small of her back when she sidled close.

About me? The wind from the door, still ajar, bellowed her jacket, but Ann stood firm. She was totally baffled.

Harry's gray brows knitted. "It's sure terrible what happened to you."

Ann shot a questioning look at Nick. "For me and for the people I should know and don't remember," she answered distractedly. Why would Nick reveal her problem to the doorman?

"Bet it is. I wondered why you were acting—" He stopped himself as if he believed he were stepping over some invisible boundary.

Ann snapped a look at him. "You wondered what?" she urged.

He hesitated, looking almost bashful suddenly. "See, like I was telling the detective, you always stopped and talked to me, asked me about my grandchildren or my wife, or we'd talk about basketball."

With unseeing eyes, she stared at the shiny marble floor. *Harry. Basketball.* She heard herself laughing with him. She saw herself with him right here in this lobby. How could she have forgotten? She used to go to games whenever possible. One night she'd had a terrible row with Redmond because he'd refused to go, and she'd given the valued tickets to Harry. Ann swayed back against the wall with the realization that she remembered being with Redmond. "Oh, Harry." She laughed at how easily that memory had returned.

"Are you okay?"

"I'm getting better every day." Memories were near, very near. Was this why Nick had left? Had he wanted to give her time alone, hoping that she'd find some small piece of her past life? Because of him, she'd made a connection with someone from her past who wasn't family or a friend, a man she'd sought friendliness with. And a fragment of a memory had slipped in unexpectedly. "I remembered fighting with Redmond about going to a basketball game," she told Nick the moment they stepped outside.

That particular memory roused Nick's grin for only an instant. "So you remember him?"

Ann shook her head. "No, not really. I had a flash of memory, of angry words about that. I saw his face, felt the anger, but nothing else." She slid her hand in his. "How did you know to talk to Harry?"

With the turn of her head, Nick caught a whiff of an alluring and expensive fragile scent. "Cop's instincts. Every time we saw him, he got this look." Nick didn't add he'd understood it.

Ann hooked her arm with his as they made their way over the slick sidewalk to his car. "What look?"

"Like you were snubbing him."

Ann said nothing about his comment, but she wondered if personal experience during his marriage had made him so attuned to the man's feelings. On a shiver, she rushed into his car. Before he flicked on the ignition, she swayed toward him for a kiss. "Did I tell you that I missed you?" she asked against his lips.

Nick couldn't be anything but honest with her. "I missed you, too."

A rush of pleasure swept quickly through Ann. She'd needed to hear him say that. Her lips still carrying the warmth of his, she twisted away to buckle her seat belt. "My grandmother called to offer me use of one of the family vehicles. So I'll need to get a driver's license." The eyes staring at her were suddenly so serious. "What is it?"

Draping an arm over the steering wheel, Nick shifted toward her. He took her hand and stared at the finger lacking an engagement ring. Wouldn't she be amazed to know he battled his own confusion every minute of the day? Even as he loved her and wanted her in his life, he sought out bits of information that promised to take her further from him. He'd spoken to her about choices, but he had none. For her sake, for a promise he'd made to himself, he had to help her remember. "We might have that for you. Your purse was found by good old Horace," he said, referring to the ranger they'd met in the woods.

"My purse was found?" Her pulse quickened at her throat. A purse. That might seem like such a trivial thing to someone else, but she felt an eagerness to touch something tangible that she'd had with her before her amnesia.

Chapter Nine

Twenty minutes later, they were strolling down the gloomy precinct hallway. All morning, Nick had pondered over Redmond Harper. During a quiet moment in the shower with the soothing water rushing over him, he'd admitted that having to watch Harper politely paw her had motivated a plan. "You might as well know. I planned to come here this morning to find out if Harper has a rap sheet."

Ann shrugged with genuine indifference. Did he think she'd care, be offended? How could she be? Except for one brief memory of Redmond, he was an unknown to her. According to what she'd gathered from her cousin's high opinion of Redmond, the Harpers' name, no doubt, was listed on the social register. She doubted Nick would find a police record for him.

When they neared the squad room, Nick dug into his pocket for coins. "It's cold. Want to get some coffee?" he asked as a diversion so he'd have time alone with Riley to fill him in on the latest information about Ann.

Ann thought the request odd from a man who'd held her coat and always opened doors for her. "Be right back."

While she wandered toward the vending machine in a corner of the hallway, Nick weaved a path to his desk. As he expected, Riley was practically prone, slouched on his chair, booted feet propped on his desk. "Pay attention," he said, knocking Riley's feet off the desk. In a few sentences, he summarized his impression of Redmond Harper. "What bothers me is that they're supposed to marry in a few weeks."

"Knew you were getting hooked on her."

"Forget that. Before we left, the grandmother said that they weren't supposed to marry until the end of the year and unexpectedly pushed their wedding date forward, even forgoing a gala event for a smaller one. Why the hurry suddenly?"

"They were hot for each other."

"God, I hope not," Nick practically snarled. "I think something else was going on."

"You're such a suspicious SOB," Riley gibed. "I'll see what I can find out about that," he assured Nick, looking past him.

Nick assumed by Riley's grin that Ann was approaching.

"Here's your coffee," she said, holding out a disposable cup to Nick.

Standing, Riley reached for the cup. "Thanks." He set it on his desk and grabbed her hand. "I'm Riley. The good cop."

Drawn to the blue eyes sparkling with friendly acceptance, Ann greeted him warmly. "I'm Ann."

"Just pretend I'm not here," Nick teased while shuffling manilla folders for the name of a woman who worked in another department.

"Thought we were." Riley led Ann into discussion about Nick's imitation of Caruso.

Her laugh, soft and airy, pulled Nick's gaze back to them. To see her smile, he was willing to let them have a few laughs at his expense. Taking advantage of an opportunity to slip away, he hounded the woman in records, hanging over her while her fingers danced across the computer keyboard.

Ann liked Riley immediately. He never asked one question. Lighthearted and easygoing, he flashed his boyish grin and related a few tales about his and Nick's rookie years on vice. "We barged right into the room. Nailed the john, got the hooker. Before Nick handcuffed the john, he handed him his pants. A high-ranking city official," he added with good humor and a wink. "I was right beside him when it happened. We had the worst duty for the next three months. Midnight tour, checking warehouses down by the docks like security guards."

"There you were working hard, and no one appreciated your efforts," Ann said, aware that the people she felt most comfortable with were Nick's family and friend.

Riley's grin broadened. "When you came in I said

to myself, now there's a woman with an understanding heart.''

Nearing them, Nick took pleasure in Ann laughing with his friend. ''Hey, what's going on?''

''He's telling all your secrets.'' In need of a rest room, Ann collected empty coffee cups to drop into a waste receptacle by the vending machine. ''I'll be back in a moment if you tell me where the women's…''

Nick offered a direction. ''Turn left at the end of the corridor.'' Still annoyed with his findings, he scowled at Riley when Ann disappeared from view. ''Harper's clean. No warrants or arrests. Only one speeding ticket in the past three years.''

''And she's a class act,'' Riley responded, apparently fishing for information about Nick's feelings.

Nick perched on the edge of his desk and spotted a crumpled pack of cigarettes in Riley's wastebasket. He'd started smoking again after his love life with a special lady had gone downhill. Love wasn't what all those songs promised.

Pushing back his chair, Riley tugged open a desk drawer and retrieved a butterscotch from his stash of hard candy. ''She doesn't remind me of Julia.''

Nick decided the trouble with good friends was that they read minds. ''Yeah, I know she doesn't.'' Shrugging, he stepped away before his friend could offer his opinion. He didn't need someone else telling him he'd be stupid to walk away from her. He knew that. But he was no dreamer. Nice as Felicia Somerset was, was she any different from Julia's family? She'd expect her granddaughter to hook up with some nice blue-blooded male who traveled in the same circle. Unfortunately that guy already existed in Ann's life.

The purse Riley had handed Ann before she left the squad room with Nick could have belonged to a stranger. More than once, while Nick drove, Ann examined the contents within the expensive leather shoulder bag. She'd hoped for more than a wallet, a comb, keys, a compact, a lipstick and pepper spray.

She handled the wallet again, opening it to stare at her driver's license. The photo matched the face she saw in a mirror, so why didn't she remember going for her license, having her photo taken? Why didn't any of her possessions look familiar? "This didn't help."

"It would have. You'd have known your name sooner."

Ann shoved the wallet back into her purse and dropped it on the floor by her feet. Enough. She'd drive herself crazy with questions. "What are we going to do now?" Yesterday she'd requested one more day. She knew he couldn't give it to her now, but she'd take what she could, even if it was only a few hours, a few blessed hours to relax.

"Plenty of snow," Nick said when she cast a look at him.

Minutes later, she moaned as he snagged her hand and they plodded around knee-high drifts in the nearby park. "We could do something else."

To Nick's way of thinking, the cold air kept the mind alert and passion subdued. "Ever build a snowman?"

"Of course." Well, she thought she probably had.

Nick smiled as she bent over and, with childlike enthusiasm, grabbed a handful of snow. She deserved moments like this, carefree time to ease troubled thoughts. If he could do nothing else, he'd do this for her.

"I suppose you think that's a masterpiece," Ann said minutes later, standing back and eyeing the bottom of the paunchy snowman he'd started.

"I'd guarantee I've made more of these than you have," Nick muttered while he packed snow on it.

Air stinging her cheeks, Ann knelt in the snow and shoved some at the smaller mound. She'd done this before. She was sure, but she sensed the experience had happened long ago. "We don't have anything for the nose or eyes."

"No imagination," Nick quipped, and grinned in response to the withering look she sent him. While he ambled to a winter-bare tree and snapped off twigs, rosy cheeked, she smoothed out lumps on the snowman. She looked young and lighthearted with the wind tossing her hair. There had been times, because she put up a good pretense, that he'd forgotten— wanted to forget—the uncertainty she faced from moment to moment, but he didn't doubt it haunted her. Breaking a stick, he wandered back to her and plugged a pointed nose on the snowman before retrieving two pennies from his pocket. The snowman's coppery eyes glittered under the sunlight. "There. It's finished."

Ann stood in front of him and scrutinized the snowman. "It's okay, but it needs a hat."

"He's fine." Turning, he packed snow in his gloves, then tossed it at her back.

As he expected, she whipped around. He read one emotion in her face—surprise. Before he could blink, youthful amusement danced in her eyes. "That's war," she declared, bending over to ball snow between her gloved hands.

Nick cracked a grin. "Yeah."

On a laugh, Ann took off after him. He was quick. Sidestepping her, he sent her sprawling in the snow with him. As she giggled, she snatched a breath before he pinned her beneath him.

"Aren't you cold?" Touching his lips to hers, he savored a sweetness that he never seemed to get enough of.

"Getting warmer," Ann murmured against his mouth.

Need blended with his yearning for her. He tasted a promise and a demand in her mouth. For now, for these moments, this had to be enough.

"I can think of something else to do," Ann whispered in his ear.

Nick chuckled while drawing her to a stand with him. "I love the way you think." He caught her at the waist and hustled her toward his car.

Briefly they stopped to brush snow from each other before entering it. With a shiver, Ann rubbed her hands together, warming them in front of the car's heater. Deliberately he'd offered her some time free of tension. She'd thought she'd be satisfied with an hour or two; she wasn't. "Do you like Chinese food?"

Nick eased the car onto the street. "Is that what you want to eat?"

"I think I like Chinese."

She looked so pleased at being able to say that. "Okay. I'll drop you off at home, stop for Chinese and bring it to your place."

Ann cast another look at him. Was this the inconsequential conversation of lovers, of people totally at ease with each other? At one time, she'd thought she might be in love with him. She had no doubts anymore. She loved him. She wanted some day to revisit that cabin with him, to eat chili and listen to rain pelting on the roof and make love beside the fire. "If I have a choice, I'll go with you."

Nick considered another errand. Negotiating several turns first, he steered the car into a parking lot. "I have to stop for a few groceries first. Want another adventure?"

Ann angled a questioning look at him. "You don't think I've ever gone grocery shopping?"

"Do you?" Nick whipped into a parking space. "Isn't there someone named Ramona?"

Ann popped out of the car, slamming her door in unison with him. "She called long-distance yesterday." At the urging of his hand, she quickened her stride to reach the warmth of the building. A stranger's voice in broken English had shared her worries about an ill brother. "She'd wanted—" Ann paused, recalling that the woman had begged for more time off to stay in Mexico. "She'd wanted to stay with her brother a little longer."

Nick yanked a grocery cart from a line of many.

"It felt odd, knowing I was her employer," she said, strolling down an aisle with him. She'd agreed to the woman's request without hesitation, for her sake as well as Ramona's. She'd wanted to avoid time with another stranger. Aware Nick had stopped, she viewed the shelves filled with cereal boxes. "What do you need?"

"We need everything."

We. She wondered if he was aware he'd said that.

By the time they packed groceries in the trunk, Ann guessed that might have been her first stop in a grocery store. That wasn't true of the video store. While Nick hung out in the action-adventure section, she wandered to the shelves lined with comedy videos.

Before they left, they settled on one of each.

"I want you to know that I compromised." Ann looked down as he took her keys and handed her the bags of Chinese food they'd picked up on the way to her apartment. "But next time we get a romance."

"This is a romance," he said, stilling in opening her apartment door to tap a finger at the video bag she was clutching to her chest.

"It's more an action adventure."

Bringing her to his side, Nick nuzzled her neck. "I've seen it before. It all starts because of his love for a woman."

"How long is she in the movie?"

"The first two minutes." He heard her laugh and gathered her to him. Though only their lips touched, he kissed her deeply until they were both breathless.

"I've made my point." Ann sighed against his mouth. "It's an action adventure."

Matching her smile, Nick pivoted away to unlock the door. "You win."

Would she? she wondered with the warmth of his mouth lingering on hers. How different would everything between them be now if they'd never learned of Redmond's existence in her life? If only...

"Give me those," Nick urged, reaching for the bags in her arms.

Snapped from her thoughts, Ann heard the trill of the phone. She dumped the bags into his opened arms and rushed to answer it. "I'll be only a minute," she called to his back as he headed for the kitchen.

After a cheery hello to her grandmother, she wandered with the phone in her hand to join him. On a long sigh, she eyed the fortune cookies he'd unpacked. Maybe they could tell her her future. Right now, she was stymied.

Nick looked up from sampling the ginger chicken. The smile had fled from her eyes. Got a problem? he mouthed.

She hated this. She wanted to be with him, yet she didn't want to hurt her grandmother's feelings. Ann clamped her hand over the mouthpiece. "It's my grandmother. She wants me to come to dinner—tonight."

He didn't hesitate—not even a second. "Go. You need to be with her."

"We have dinner already here and..."

With a fingertip, beneath her chin, he slanted her face up so he could see her eyes. "We'll eat this for breakfast."

Emotion poured out of her. She understood what

he was doing for her. She needed to find her past. Her future—any that she might long for with him—would elude her until she did that. "Yes, I'll be there," she said to her grandmother. "Seven-thirty." She listened a moment longer before saying goodbye. Setting the phone on the counter, she sighed heavily. "Now I wish that I had refused."

Nick paused in closing the cartons. Hell, he wasn't too happy, either, but more important than them was her. She needed to find her way back to herself. "Why the lack of enthusiasm?"

"I had it until she told me Redmond and Stephanie would be there. Then it was too late to think of a way to refuse."

The fiancé. He presented another problem. He belonged in Ann's life. And Nick was having a damn hard time remembering that. In passing, he skimmed her hip with his fingertips. "I'm taking an egg roll to go." Because he couldn't resist, he kissed her cheek.

She didn't let him get to the door. "Nick?"

A hand on the doorknob, he pivoted back to her. "Yeah?"

Ann crossed to him and curled her arms around his neck. "I'll be by later."

"I'll be waiting." What else could he do now? he wondered.

Dinner at her grandmother's included fine bone china and Waterford crystal. Earlier Ann had enjoyed the time alone with her grandmother in the library as Felicia had filled her in on her love of one horse, an Arabian named Thunder. The idea of riding a horse had seemed unfamiliar, but her grandmother had assured her she loved to ride. They'd hunched over a photograph album. Not even those of her parents had sparked recognition. She looked like her mother, she'd learned. As a child, she'd had a cat. Whatever else she might have uncovered ended abruptly when Redmond arrived for dinner.

While they ate soup, he bragged about his tennis skill. The word *I* played an important part in his conversations. More interested in the plate before her, Ann tuned him out and brushed her fingertips across the two delicate miniature flowers on the china. It even had gold trim at the rim. Fragments of inconsequential facts came easily. Why did important ones elude her? Was her mind shielding her from something too painful to face? She knew now she hadn't been abused or threatened. Her life hadn't been in danger, so what could have been so devastating to her?

"Gillian?"

Ann raised her gaze from her plate of salmon and steamed vegetables. By the scowl on Redmond's face, she assumed he'd been trying to get her attention.

"I told my uncle we'd be able to stay with him at his castle for several days while we're on our honeymoon in England."

Ann remained silent. Was he taking advantage of her, aware she was lost every minute he'd been talking? Until she understood herself better, could she challenge anything anyone said?

At her lack of response, Redmond scowled with displeasure. "I thought you'd be pleased."

It was impossible to keep a trace of resentment from her voice. "There's so much to consider. I'm not sure I want to—"

"Of course, you're terribly confused," he interrupted.

Ann rankled. "Redmond, I may be confused because I can't remember, but I am capable of making decisions."

His brows knitted, but he made no comment.

As they finished their coffee and cherries jubilee, Ann wondered what was next. Somehow she dodged Redmond's suggestion that they get their coats and stroll outside. "It's cold," she said as an excuse.

"You always preferred cold weather."

He was right. She did like walking in the snow, but she thought he needed a reminder. "I'm not the same anymore."

"You'll be yourself again soon," he said with a firmness that indicated he expected just that.

To her relief, within the hour, he announced that he had to leave because of a business meeting. Ann watched his car pull away, then ambled along the hallway upstairs. Was he always so overbearing, or was it her own confusion making her see him in such an unflattering way?

Wondering which room had been hers, she opened the first door at the top of the landing. A maid turned a look back on her. Ann stilled, riveted to the photograph of a woman on the bedside table.

"Beautiful, too, your mother was," the maid said with a trace of Irish brogue. "The Mrs. Ann was so proud when she had you. She laughed kind of musical like when she chose your name. Saying she was that Gillian was so much prettier than her own."

Ann. Her mother's name had been Ann. Why hadn't her grandmother told her that? Annoyed, she descended the staircase. She hit the bottom one to see her grandmother in the library with a tall, white-haired man.

"Stephanie had a dozen phone calls to make," Felicia said, before introducing Ann to the family doctor. "I hope you don't mind, but I wanted to make sure you were all right."

How could she be upset with someone whose only concern was her well-being?

The examination was painless and short. He checked where the bump had been and smiled. "Your physical injury was minor." He offered words that she'd heard before, "Take your time. Memory will come back to you."

She returned a smile that took effort as he wandered with her grandmother to the door to leave. She was tired of being patient. Rising from the settee, she crossed to the window and waited until she heard the hum of her grandmother's wheelchair again.

"Redmond annoyed you this evening. I suppose he feels you have a need for more guidance since your amnesia."

"Did he always like to control everything?"

Felicia remained expressionless. "Yes, but you'd never allow him to."

Ann was glad to hear that.

Her grandmother moved her wheelchair to the

desk. "We could play cards, gin rummy. That's something we did often whenever you came to visit."

Smiling, Ann settled on a chair near her. "Another night?"

"Of course." Felicia took her hand. "I'm so glad you're here."

"I like being with you," Ann said honestly. She watched pleasure brighten her grandmother's eyes. "Will you help me?" she asked almost pleadingly. "I know you want to protect me, but you're the only one who can tell me about my parents. It's important for me to know the woman I was, the girl who grew up in this house."

It was close to midnight when Ann used the key Nick had given her and unlocked the front door of his house. Since his car was parked in the driveway, she expected to find him lounged on his favorite chair in the living room. The room was dark.

Without turning on lights, she made her way to the kitchen to see him with hands plunged in dishwater. "Hi," she said from the doorway. He turned slowly with suds clinging to his hands. She went to him, not to lean on him but because she needed to touch him. She needed the solidness he represented, the calm that drifted over her when she was around him.

"Hi, yourself." Nick dried his hands. When she stepped near, he set his fingers lightly on the sharp points of her hips, and bent his head for a kiss. Her soft sigh of pleasure relaxed him. "It got so late that I thought you'd go home."

This is home, she nearly said. "I needed someone to talk to."

He considered that a compliment. He'd watched his parents often, trying to understand what had made their marriage work. He'd come to one conclusion. Beyond the love and the passion, they were friends, able to share their thoughts with each other. He never thought he'd feel that for any woman before he met Ann. Moving behind her, he held the collar of her coat while she slid out of the sleeves. For a second, he rested his cheek against her cold temple. "How was the fiancé?" He'd had to ask. All night he'd made himself face facts. Eventually she'd remember Harper.

As she tilted her face toward him, his breath, warm and tempting, mingled with hers. "Don't ask about him." How simple her life had been days ago. Wonderfully simple. Fatigue swept over her as she sank to a chair. "My grandmother told me about my parents. I don't think she really wanted to."

Stepping away to pour her coffee, Nick sympathized with Felicia. Protectiveness came with loving someone. Often enough he'd had to stifle his own for Ann.

"She said that I was really close to my father, probably because it was hard for me to reach out to my mother. By the way, her name was Ann."

Nick set a cup of coffee in front of her before taking a nearby seat. "No wonder you chose that one."

Nodding, Ann went on. "She was sickly and not really approachable. My grandmother said that my father tried to be understanding, but it wasn't easy."

"He wasn't understanding of your mother's sickness?"

"It wasn't physical. It was mental. She was jealous, sometimes irrational." Ann gazed at the dark liquid in her cup. "I don't remember her. I don't remember any of that."

Nick closed his hand over hers. "You might have blocked it all out before the amnesia because it was painful for you."

"No, my grandmother said I never forgot. I was supposed to be at the stables all afternoon for a riding lesson. My father promised to be home for it, but he called later that day and said he couldn't make it." Ann sipped her coffee. "My grandmother was—was so reluctant to talk about them, as if she didn't want to tell me anything."

He tried to imagine the little girl she'd been. "So you went to the riding lesson?"

"Yes, I did, but I forgot a carrot for the horse." She smiled weakly. "Thunder. His name was Thunder, and I loved him. So I ran back to the house. The maid was there, but my mother and grandmother were at a relative's and, like I said, my father was at the office. I got the carrot and ran upstairs for—"

Nick raised a halting hand. "Wait a minute. Do you remember this?"

"No." Ann met his eyes. "The maid told my grandmother what happened. I needed to use the washroom, so I ran upstairs. Later, I told my grandmother that I had heard sounds, and I walked down the hallway to my parents' bedroom. I saw my father in bed with another woman."

Nick frowned. A heavy-duty scene for a little girl who thought her father was perfect. He'd disappointed her, maybe she even viewed his choosing time with the woman instead of her as rejection.

"According to my grandmother, I was devastated."

"What happened with your father?" he asked.

"I turned away from him. It's strange. It sounds so sad, but I feel as if it happened to someone else."

Nick wanted to gather her close. He required no degree in psychology to see that a little girl's trust in the person she loved most of all had been destroyed.

"I don't understand the woman my family talks about, who spent so much time shopping, who attended parties and traveled." As his fingertip touched her chin, she tilted her head back. "She seems like a stranger to me, Nick. Someone I'm not sure I like."

Nick didn't miss the plea in her eyes. Even if that time in her childhood eluded her, she'd had a rough evening, listening to the unhappiness she'd lived through. "Give her time. She might grow on you."

"Is that what I did with you?"

Hunching closer, he caressed her lips with his own. "From the moment I first saw you."

Chapter Ten

Morning sunlight filtered into the bedroom. Groggy with sleep, Nick took a moment to orient himself, struggling to awaken. On a low groan, he rolled to his back and opened his eyes. Her stark white bedroom reminded him of a hospital room. Last night he'd driven her home. He hadn't planned to stay. Then she'd stepped into his arms, and the ache had begun.

It came easily, too easily. It rippled through him now as she shifted to sit on the edge of the mattress, offering him a view of a back as slim and flawless as the rest of her.

"Are you trying to entice me to curl up to you again?" she asked on a soft laugh in response to the finger he was running sensuously slowly up her spine.

Placing a gentle hand on her shoulder, he urged her down beside him. "Definitely."

With the caress of his mouth at a sensitive spot beneath her earlobe, Ann went with sensation and closed her eyes. "I love when you—" Softly she moaned in response to the ringing phone. "Don't forget where you were."

Possessively he stroked a hand down her hip. "Never."

Amusement colored her voice as she greeted the caller. "No, I was awake," she said in response to her grandmother's question. That certainly wasn't a lie. Her senses hummed with the promise of Nick's caresses. "Yes, I'm having lunch with Sara. She mentioned Stephanie and someone named Trish." At her grandmother's comment, Ann worked up enthusiasm. "Oh, she's a cousin of Redmond's. Yes, I'll enjoy seeing her again."

Though she sounded lighthearted, Nick noticed her fingers tightening on the receiver.

"Thank you. Yes, I will," Ann answered before saying goodbye. "My grandmother," she said, dropping the receiver back in its cradle. On a laugh, as Nick tugged at her, she fell back. Her head on his shoulder, she turned her face to kiss his chest. The yearning blossomed within her for the touch of his hands on her. "What time do you have to testify in court?"

"Later," he assured her, and rolled her with him.

Around ten they finished breakfast. "We were supposed to eat last night's dinner this morning." Plates in one hand, Ann stretched and flicked off the radio and a bluesy tune by Mariah Carey.

"I'm more sensible than that."

Maybe too sensible. She wished he'd let her and himself go with their feelings. She supposed that was impossible. "Someone wants you," she said at the sound of his beeper.

You, I hope. Nick kept the words to himself and punched out a telephone number. He laughed at the urgency in another detective's voice as he explained the reason for his call.

Ann folded a dish towel and looked at him, drawn to the rush of amusement in his voice.

"Nine-year-olds? Yeah, I'll do it. You'd better be assistant-coaching." Nick laughed again before saying goodbye and setting the receiver back in its cradle. "Little League," he explained. "They're already recruiting coaches."

Ann set the towel aside. He was a nice man, generous with his time and his feelings. He could be quietly persuasive. He could be undeniably intimidating. He was always caring, a man who'd give without a second of thought. Unfortunately, weaved into all those fine qualities existed stubbornness. It was that trait she prepared herself to battle.

In two days, he would go back to work, but she recalled he'd said he had one Saturday night off, this coming one. "Will you come to a party with me Saturday night?" In her mind, she belonged with no one except him.

"What kind of party?"

"It's my cousin Stephanie's birthday. That's why

my grandmother called. To remind me. Please go with me," she appealed. Without understanding his reluctance, she could only make assumptions. "Because of Julia, are you uncomfortable at my grandmother's house?"

Nick moved away from the phone. An explanation seemed impossible, but she deserved one. "Sit. We'll talk." Ghosts of the past, of a time with Julia, still haunted him, he realized. "The problem with Julia had nothing to do with the money," he said when he settled beside her at the table.

Ann didn't understand. "But you said that her parents—"

"They did, but the money wasn't the problem. It was the way they acted because of their wealth that put me on edge."

Shifting on the seat, Ann inclined her head. Was she unfairly opening an old wound?

"About a week before the final blowup, her father offered me a job. Told me I should leave the police force. No Wainwright had ever had a public servant's job. Emphasis on servant."

In the short time Ann had known him, she'd learned of his pride in being a policeman.

"I told him that I wasn't a Wainwright." Nick laughed mirthlessly. "He looked at me as if I had dropped in from another planet. And he told me that, of course, I would have a proper position with his company. I'd learned to read between the lines with them. That meant I'd make lots of money so I could keep their little girl happy, but I wouldn't have any responsibility. Well, I refused. And Julia threw a tantrum.''

Ann toyed with a napkin on the table. He'd known pain, far more than he revealed.

"We were all letting go with some tough words, and I guess Julia sensed I wasn't backing down. I don't think any Wainwright had ever been refused before. A few days later, I overheard a conversation between Julia and a friend. She said she was bored with marriage. She'd considered the time with me a nice adventure.''

Ann viewed them as hurtful words. Pride-wrenching ones.

"Over dinner that evening, somewhere between the escargot and the salad.'' Nick paused, grateful now that he could find a smidgen of amusement in that time of his life. "Anyway, when I confronted her, she admitted that she'd married me impulsively because her parents objected to me. She'd been rebelling against her family.'' He couldn't say some of her words, her last ones that had sliced through him. "She said she wanted a divorce. She was tired of being married to a peasant who couldn't give her a life-style she was used to.''

Ann wanted to hold him, to comfort him, even though he was past needing it. The woman didn't know what she'd lost. As far as she was concerned, now that he'd told her about that time in his life, only one question needed answering. "Do you think I'm like her?''

God, he knew she wasn't. She'd been the one who'd lightened his bitterness, who'd made him believe in love again. "No." Nick leaned close and smoothed back her hair in a reassuring gesture.

"Then go with me."

"I know you're scared, but what do you think everyone will say if I'm there?"

Ann recognized his noble act. He was refusing for her sake. This was about what he thought was best for her, not his feelings. "I'm not going without you."

"You have to go to see how others react to you. To see if someone sparks memories. Don't be a victim of your own fear."

"You don't understand." It wasn't a matter of needing him with her. "I'm not afraid to be alone. I want you with me."

Want, not need. One word clouded his good reason. True, the cop in him couldn't walk away until he had all the answers. But it was the man who loved her who answered. "I'll go," he said, standing and pulling her into his arms.

"Black tie," Ann whispered close to his ear, and laughed when he moaned.

She'd gone the simple route, she realized. She'd leaned on him. But didn't love mean having someone to help shoulder burdens, someone to share joys with? If he didn't realize that, would he have agreed to go with her? Love. It existed between them. Whether he said the words or not, he kept telling her in the way he acted. She had to believe that he loved her.

While Nick sat in a courtroom fending off questions from a defense attorney, she was standing in front of her closet, combating indecisiveness while she searched for something appropriate to wear to lunch with friends. Debating about which outfit was suitable, she tossed several of them on the bed. Her inability to make a decision was driving her crazy. Uneasiness fluttered through her whenever she thought about the meeting. What would she talk to them about?

That was the wrong attitude, wasn't it? Instead of being nervous, she should use this luncheon to her advantage. Friends would know about her. She could learn a lot from them. With the pep talk delivered, she chose winter white pants and a steel blue sweater.

Two hours later she met Sara and Stephanie and the third in their trio, Trish Burns. Needing some kind of security surrounding her, Ann suggested Vincetti's for lunch.

"This is quaint," Stephanie murmured with undisguised disdain when they were seated.

"Unusual," Trish added, subtly rolling her eyes. She was a slim woman with shiny brown hair. She'd hugged Ann warmly, then had begun chattering about a duke she'd met while on the Riviera. She hadn't stopped talking since. "Nothing like slumming," she said suddenly, and not too softly, while examining the spotless silverware in front of her.

Ann wrestled with annoyance. Were they always so snide? Discreetly she looked around, hoping none of Nick's family had heard. After their kindness to her, offending any of them was the last thing she wanted to do.

"You really haven't changed," Sara said with a trace of amusement.

Ann believed she was different from the woman they knew. A blank mind forced rediscovery, had made her question her attitudes and values.

"You always did what you wanted," Sara informed her. "Poor Redmond."

As she laughed, so did the others.

Everyone knew the joke but Ann. "What about him?"

Trish took over, laughing as she spoke. "You tugged him into one of those ghastly little quick-stop markets for these incredibly awful brownies, the ones that are covered with gooey frosting. It was simply hilarious, darling. He was mortified. He claimed his taste buds revolted simply from watching you eat one."

Ann struggled to fix a smile on her face during the rest of the luncheon. It wasn't easy. The last bite of fettucini alfredo balled in her throat because of what they'd just told her.

"Men who are more interested in our money than us is a problem we all have," Trish added on a sigh.

Sara arched a brow at Trish. "I didn't know your family had any of their own."

Trish's lips pursed at her friendly snideness. "We are direct descendants of several influential men of the American Revolution," she returned in a haughty manner that resembled Redmond's.

A genetic curse, Ann supposed.

"We're discussing money, not lineage."

"Now, I see why we're here. The scenery is absolutely awe inspiring," Trish purred.

Ann followed her stare to the door, to Nick. His brows drawn together, he offered no smile.

"My, that is delicious," Trish continued.

Sara stretched to the side to see past Trish. "That one belongs to Gillian."

Ann felt out of synch with the women around her. Sara had sounded as if they collected men for amusement. Then what? When bored with the man of the hour, did they discard him and move on to a new one? Suddenly struck with weariness, she wanted to go to Nick and step out the door.

"He belongs to Gillian?" Trish briefly dragged her gaze from Nick. "You know him?"

Sara arched a brow. "He's the gorgeous policeman grabbing Gillian's attention these days. I told you about him."

"He's *that* one?" Trish sighed loudly. "Why is it that I never meet any distractions who look like that?"

Ann tucked her tongue to restrain anger. The lunch was almost over.

"We must do this soon." Standing, Trish collected her purse and fur jacket, then bent over and brushed cheeks with Ann. "There's a marvelous gallery opening next Friday."

"I heard about it," Sara responded, saving Ann from having to respond.

"We'll all go," Trish insisted. "*I'll* choose where we have lunch though. Nice as the scenery is, Gillian, this is simply too plebeian to suit me."

The others nodded like puppets whose strings had been pulled.

When the door shut behind them, Ann leaned back in her chair on a long sigh. She felt like a mechanical doll, smiling and responding at appropriate moments. Before, she must have been close to them. They knew so much about her. So why was it difficult to feel that friendship? Why did their manner annoy her? Had she changed that much from the woman Gillian Somerset had been? Maybe she wasn't as confused as she thought. It seemed to her she was viewing life and the people around her through a much clearer lens.

Reaching for her wineglass, she stared at the third finger of her left hand. An engagement ring had been there. Where had it gone? And what was she going to do about a fiancé she didn't remember, much less love?

"Are you ready to leave?"

Deep in thought, Ann jumped, sloshing the wine in her glass. "Nick."

Settling beside her, he stared hard, trying to determine her mood. She didn't look happy, not one bit. "Was it a difficult lunch?"

Keeping anything from him seemed foolish. "In more ways than you might think." Ann feigned laughter. "I was told I've always had a liking for those gooey cupcakes. And I didn't always behave properly."

For the moment, Nick rode on the hint of forced humor he heard in her voice. "How reassuring."

Her attempt at a smile failed. "I dumped a bowl of caviar on one man's head."

Since that seemed uncharacteristic for her, Nick wanted to know why she'd done it, yet he didn't ask. "Guess he irritated you."

Lightly she ran a fingertip around the rim of her wineglass. "So I was told."

"Got a secret?" he asked, inclining his head to force her to look at him.

Hadn't she had a similar thought because her friends had been so reluctant to tell her why she'd acted like that? She'd been annoyed, feeling as if they were taunting her with bits and pieces of information about Mark Tolbin.

"Was this guy important?"

"According to them, yes. I was nearly engaged to him. He was marvelously talented—an artist. Trish's description. But poor, Stephanie had said." Try as she might, Ann couldn't even picture the man in her mind. "It seems that I met him while I was on a ski vacation at Vail and was infatuated with him. My family wasn't."

Nick narrowed his eyes. This tale sounded too familiar. "What did they do about him?"

How naïve she was, Ann realized. He'd instinctively made an assumption that hadn't entered her mind when Trish had been talking. "You assumed they did something?"

"Money wields power."

"Yes," she admitted. "And he was offered money to leave me alone."

Nick laced his fingers with hers. Some man had hurt her badly. She might not remember him, but the wound was inside her, maybe still festering. "And he took it," he said, rather than asked.

"According to them, I was heartbroken when his true intentions were revealed."

His eyes never left her face. "Not a good memory." With a trusting heart, she'd offered love and had been deceived again.

"I don't remember him, which I guess I should be thankful for since I was obviously humiliated." Clear to her though was that distrust had controlled her past. She'd narrowed her choices to men she knew, men with their own money. Redmond is a marvelous catch, Stephanie had insisted during lunch. Ann had yet to find the attractive qualities in Redmond beneath his narcissistic personality, but she assumed he must possess some.

"What about the fiancé who's around now? Did they tell you anything about him?"

"It was all complimentary."

"Wonderful," Nick murmured.

Ann enjoyed the flash of what appeared to be jealousy that flared in his dark eyes. "He's smooth, persuasive, shrewd. Again, that's Stephanie's description."

"Has she got a thing for him?"

"I wondered that, too, but she seemed too encouraging for me to marry him for that to be true."

Even a mention of that marriage carried a kick. Nick drew a deep breath to ease the knot in his stomach. "What else did they say about him?" Deep down, he hoped to learn something that would lead him in an investigation of Harper. Ten to twenty years locked up would suit Nick fine.

"He has quite a reputation for being a shrewd businessman because of a land deal in Florida."

"Tell me about it."

"He was working for his uncle in Florida and managed to sell some undeveloped land from his family's holdings."

"To a corporation?"

"No, individuals—retirees." Ann had thought it all sounded terribly deceitful, but none of the others had seemed to view it that way.

"Useless land?" Nick asked.

Ann nodded. By the look in Nick's eyes, he wasn't too impressed with Redmond's salesmanship, either. "I'm going to call my grandmother. I'm sure she can tell me more about Mark Tolbin."

"Why do you want to know more?"

"I'm wondering what kind of woman could be so fooled by a man."

Nick cupped the base of her neck and massaged lightly. "You're too hard on yourself. Everyone can play the fool at some time or another." He'd done a top-notch job of it himself with another woman.

As he drew her to a stand with him, she shunned the humiliation nagging her since she'd learned about Mark Tolbin. "I'm ready to leave." She roused a smile for him. "But I need to talk to your mother first."

"My mother?" Nick turned a curious expression on her. "Why?"

Ann was bound and determined to prove something not only to him but also herself. "*This* is a secret."

Something twisted within him at the sight of her eyes dancing with a smile. "Okay," he said, going along with whatever she had planned. "When you come out, I'll walk you to your car." While she rushed into the kitchen, Nick followed his sister's movements. A hand at her back, Bianca sought the chair closest to the cash register. Though his pregnant sister no longer waited on tables, she'd insisted on sitting-down jobs in the kitchen to help the family.

"I'm back." Lightly Ann curled fingers over his arm to get his attention. He'd seemed a million miles away. "Will I see you tonight?"

"My house," he said in a low voice. Minutes together were precious now. At some moment, she'd inch her way through that wall in her mind.

Inside the car, with a glance at the clock on the dashboard, Ann calculated she'd have enough time to make one stop before going to Nick's house.

Only the help of a sympathetic grandmotherly woman in the grocery store saved Ann from wandering from one aisle to the next. "The first time you cook a meal by yourself is always the hardest," the woman had said.

Ann repeated the woman's encouragement when she was standing in Nick's kitchen. With a shake of her head, she slouched against the kitchen counter and bit her bottom lip as she read the recipe for calzones she'd gotten from Nick's mother. She could do this. She was intelligent, capable. Most of all, she was determined, she reminded herself while she rolled out the dough.

"Knead like this." His mother had demonstrated before Ann had left the restaurant kitchen with the recipe.

For several minutes, Ann turned the dough on the well-floured board. Flour splattered on the counter and the front of her. "Okay, it says to let it rise," she murmured to herself while reading the recipe.

After cleaning off her hands on a towel, she punched out her grandmother's phone number. The butler conveyed that she'd left for an appointment at the salon. On second thought, Ann decided not reaching her grandmother was best. The conversation she wanted with her might prove more informative if they were face-to-face.

At five o'clock, with one step into the house, Nick was greeted by the scent of spices that had permeated the kitchen of his youth. "What's this?" he asked, when he reached the kitchen doorway and saw her standing at the stove.

"Dinner." While she rubbed fingers at the flour on her face, she smiled down at the calzones on a baking sheet.

"It smells great." Nuzzling her neck, he inhaled her alluring, expensive fragrance. "So do you." A longing to hold her close forever overwhelmed him. She'd spent her afternoon chopping spinach, beating ricotta, grating parmesan and rolling dough. For him. She'd done all this for him. "Thank you."

"You haven't tasted it yet," Ann reminded him on a laugh.

Nick brushed his lips across hers, more interested in her taste than any other. "Thank you anyway." He wanted her. He'd never known such need for any woman. It went beyond physical yearning. He fed on the sound of her voice, the hint of her smile. In a short time, she'd become more a part of his life than Julia ever had. Words of love clung to his tongue. Did he have a right to say them to a woman searching for herself?

"Come on." Ann grabbed his hand as she stepped back. "We'll think about dessert later."

With a laugh at himself, Nick released her hand to retrieve his best bottle of wine from a kitchen cupboard. He had it in his hand when the doorbell resounded in the air. Under his breath, he muttered as he set the bottle on the table, then crossed to the door. Romantic notions floating around in his mind, he was in no mood for company.

A second later, he wondered if he was gaping. Never had he envisioned Felicia Somerset on his front porch. "Mrs. Somerset, hello." As solemn looking as the butler, the chauffeur stood behind her wheelchair.

Wrapped in a warm fur coat, she adjusted the blanket on her lap. "May I come in?"

"Yes, of course." Nick swept open the door and shot a look over his shoulder at Ann standing in the kitchen doorway. She appeared as dumbfounded as he was.

"My granddaughter called and I—" Felicia cut off her comment as she spotted Ann. "Charles told me you'd called. However, I couldn't reach you at your apartment.''

Ann tried to look innocent. She didn't think she was succeeding.

''Since you'd given me your address after coming to see me the first time,'' she said to Nick, ''I decided to take a leisurely drive. I thought you might be here, my dear.''

Ann grinned foolishly. ''Here I am.''

''Yes, I see that.''

Nick resisted an urge to nervously shift his stance. The last time he'd felt so uneasy he'd been sixteen and crazy about Christine Chynknowski. Crazy enough to face her father, a man built like a linebacker. Aware of both women staring at him, he nearly laughed. ''Why don't you—''

''Join us. I made dinner,'' Ann said pridefully.

''Dinner?''

The woman had a great poker face. Except for one gray brow lifting slightly, she showed no reaction. With a turn of her head, she indicated to her chauffeur that she was staying.

Nick sent Ann a what-do-we-do-now look. The shoulders she shrugged in response wasn't too encouraging. He'd hoped she knew how to deal with this situation. He sure as hell didn't. ''I have coffee, but no tea.''

''He has a wonderful white wine,'' Ann interjected.

''That would be nice.''

''I'll get it,'' Nick volunteered. In passing Ann in the doorway, he blew out a long breath. This might be an evening to remember.

Chapter Eleven

Gracious, Felicia raved after she took her first bite of her granddaughter's culinary feat.

"It is good." Nick dove his fork into more of the filling.

Pleased, Ann couldn't help beaming. "You don't have to act so surprised," she teased Nick.

"Well, I tasted your French toast, remember?"

Wrinkling her nose, Ann smiled at her grandmother. "It was a little soggy."

Felicia's eyes darted from her granddaughter to Nick.

What was she thinking? Nick mused. Her granddaughter was weeks away from marrying another man.

"It's really quite good," Felicia assured Ann. "I

talked to Stephanie earlier. She said your luncheon was unusual.''

Ann had expected worse from her cousin.

''They had lunch at my family's restaurant,'' Nick said as an explanation, certain the woman was also sharp enough to interpret what that meant.

''The menu lacked vichyssoise and escargot.'' Over the rim of her wineglass, Felicia's eyes twinkled with humor. ''Don't think too harshly of them,'' she said, directing her comment to Nick. ''They have narrow vision.''

What a wonderful woman she was, Ann thought. Because she'd repeatedly displayed such sensitivity and truthfulness, Ann depended on her for details about a humiliating time in her life. ''They mentioned Mark Tolbin.''

''Why would they do that?'' her grandmother asked sharply.

''I don't think they intended to,'' Ann assured her.

''My dear, it was such a painful time for you. It's the past,'' she said, catching Ann's hand in hers.

But it was the past she needed to remember. ''I really want to know more,'' Ann insisted, steering conversation back to a man who remained faceless to her.

Nick noticed Felicia didn't even attempt to argue, as if aware that her granddaughter, like herself, possessed an iron will. When either one made a decision, that was that.

''You were seventeen years old. A child. You thought you were in love with him. You were guilt-less.''

Ann took a long breath. "Naive?"

Her grandmother's lips curved in a warm smile. "You may not remember the past, but my dear, you are my granddaughter. Gillian Somerset had a mind of her own. Just like the woman sitting across from me. Yes, you might say you were naive. I'd say you were young and innocent. He stole that innocence, your trust. He changed you."

Tightening her hand on her grandmother's, Ann hunched toward her. "In what way?"

"You became more distant. You must understand, Gillian, so much had happened to you that you viewed as rejection. Your parents let you down. Then, after that unfortunate episode with Mark Tolbin, you were extremely upset. And more cautious."

Nick broke off a slice of bread from the loaf in a basket. "What do you mean?" he prodded.

"With feelings. After that distasteful business, you trusted only a select few," she said to Ann. "Myself, Sara and Redmond."

"What about Redmond?" Ann asked, trying to understand her attraction for him. "Were we friends and I grew to love him?"

Did the earth move when they kissed? Nick wondered. It had for him.

Felicia had finished eating, and dabbed the napkin at her lips. "Not remembering him has changed your mind about the marriage?" Briefly her eyes shifted to Nick. "You postponed it once before. We could again if that's what you wish."

Rather than answer, Ann asked another question,

"Why did I postpone the wedding to him months ago?"

"I believe because of doubts."

"Did I tell you that I had doubts?" Ann asked.

"Gillian, you simply told me that there were too many plans to make to rush into it."

As Ann frowned, Nick assumed she was as confused as he was. "I thought they'd planned to get married next year and moved the date forward." Instincts always controlled him. Nothing felt right when he thought about Redmond, but he had no proof the man was anything except the unfortunate fiancé waiting for the woman he loved to remember him.

"This will require some explaining." Felicia sighed. "They'd chosen a date." She looked at her granddaughter again. "Then you said you wanted to wait until next year."

Trying to decipher whether she was telling everything, Ann studied her grandmother's eyes intensely. They were clear with truthfulness.

"However, after dinner with Redmond at the club one night, you arrived at my house, told me he was persuasive, and you were rescheduling your wedding to an earlier date."

"I seesaw a lot."

"It might seem that way, my dear. I believe you were initially concerned because Redmond was having financial difficulties for a while."

Ann stiffened. Was she as superficial as the women she'd lunched with. "So I wouldn't marry him because he couldn't give me all that I was used to?"

"No, I believe you were apprehensive. For quite a

long time after you stopped seeing Mark Tolbin, you questioned everyone's motives toward you.''

Ann read between the lines. "I wondered if Redmond was marrying me for my money.''

"Obviously you considered that not to be true or you wouldn't have agreed to a more immediate wedding date.''

As good as dinner was, Nick couldn't eat more. Too many reminders about a wedding. Standing, he took his plate and Felicia's as she set down her fork. "Mrs. Somerset, would you like coffee?''

"No, thank you, Nicholas.''

Ann slanted a look at him. She doubted she'd ever seen him look quite so surprised.

Nicholas. Nick grinned as he ambled from the dining room to the kitchen.

"You seemed so happy before we started discussing this," Felicia commented as Nick disappeared into the kitchen.

"I'm not unhappy. I wish—I wish I understood myself better," Ann admitted.

Her grandmother opened her arms to her.

Without any awkwardness, Ann clung to this fragile woman who seemed like a pillar of strength to her at the moment. When they drew apart, her grandmother smiled and stroked Ann's cheek. "I think you do.''

"I know now that trust is important to me, isn't it?''

"Yes. And it seems there is someone else you trust.''

Her grandmother meant Nick. "For a while I placed my life in his hands."

"So freely?"

"Yes," Ann admitted. "From the moment we met."

"Then he's special to you?"

"I'm in love with him."

A frown crossed Felicia's brow. "I see."

Ann expected her grandmother to offer some advice that she didn't want to hear, but Felicia said nothing in response to Ann's declaration.

"I had a lovely time. Thank you," she said later while she bundled again in her coat.

"I'll call you in the morning," Ann promised, stepping out on the porch as the chauffeur steered the wheelchair toward the stairs.

Nick stood behind Ann. He assumed the chauffeur had hefted the wheelchair up the steps alone, and decided there was no need to repeat the process. Together, they lowered the wheelchair to the sidewalk. Felicia offered another polite thank-you. Nick would have loved to be a mind reader tonight. "That was quite a surprise," he said when he followed Ann into the house. He shut the door and turned away from it to find her face inches from his. "You do know what she's thinking."

"I know she loves me. You were right about that." She responded with a smile to his lopsided grin. "I know she wants me to be happy." Sliding her hands up his back, she raised her mouth to the one that promised so much pleasure. Emotion flooded her when with this man, not another. He was the one who'd given her so much. He'd made her feel wanted. Loved.

Nick gripped her tighter as her lips parted, then touched his. He couldn't think when her mouth was on his. Fire and heat overwhelmed everything else. As if it were the first time, hunger came with breathtaking quickness. He accepted that there was no sanity in passion. Heat exploded within him. The woman in his arms, the one whose softness enticed him, the one who made him tremble was all he'd ever hoped for.

While lips clung, while kisses deepened, their hands seemed to move with a will of their own, his tugging off her blouse, hers pulling his shirt down his arms. He felt possessed. He yearned. He ached. He loved. Yeah, he loved. It had crept in on him without warning. Holding her length to his, he backed her away from the door. They got as far as the living room rug.

With a heady sigh, Ann closed her eyes. More than the seduction of his mouth and the dark male taste of him aroused her passion. As the coolness in the room whispered at her back when he slid off one strap of her bra and then the other, she drifted with a sense of completeness. With him, she felt whole.

She heard his low groan and knew her heart was already bound to the one racing with her own. As he unclasped her bra, as his hands caressed her flesh, the undeniable warmth began to spiral through her. She felt his heat and hardness and wedged a hand between them, then popped the snap of his jeans with deft fingers.

Huskily he murmured something against her throat. Ann didn't care what he'd said. She was suddenly as impatient as he. It was his touch, his kiss she craved. She wanted to speak, to tell him how she felt. She could barely breathe with his mouth nibbling now at her breasts, roaming down her body. With excruciating slowness, his teeth caught and pulled at her panties.

Knuckles grazing her belly and thighs torched the fire burning within her. Before, she had felt her heart quicken for him. Now it raced. He played on her need, stroking it. On a soft moan, she threw her head back, pressing it into the carpet, arching to meet the heat of his breath.

Her body swelled as his hands never stilled, as his tongue drove her to writhing madness. Breathless from each moist flick of his tongue, she was lost in him. Early evening air floated over her with its chill; she was hot with need when he rose above her.

His dark eyes hooded with passion, his face tight with tension, he captured her mouth again, and he lowered himself to her. With a soft cry, she urged him, offering whatever he wanted to take. Arms and legs embracing his body, she blended with him, drawing him deeper, filling herself with him, knowing this memory, like the first between them, wouldn't be the last. Without more, she'd die, she thought in a brief coherent second.

Then slowly he moved against her, and with her. Each stroke grew more demanding, more insistent until their bodies pounded to keep pace with the fever pitch of desire. As she'd done since the day they'd met, she followed his lead—willingly, unquestion-ingly, trustingly.

During the next three days, Ann juggled her time. Frazzled, she felt as if she were having a personality split. But which was the real one? The woman who laughed and loved with Nick, who'd gone bowling and country dancing, or the one who'd attended an afternoon tea at the Somerset estate, who'd made her-self go to the symphony with a fiancé who remained a stranger, who owned a wedding dress of Irish lace and satin? The first time she'd seen the gown hanging in a bedroom in her grandmother's home, she'd felt her stomach clench. The dress had symbolized how real a forthcoming marriage to Redmond was.

She let the shower spray flow over her. Lifting her face to the water, she closed her eyes and ran her fingers through soapy hair until she heard the squeak of well-rinsed hair beneath her hands, then turned off the water. Suddenly it seemed everyone wanted to fill the emptiness in her life, a life split into segments while she tried to please them. Twice, she'd attempted to tell Redmond her feelings had changed, and she'd failed. She didn't want to hurt anyone, but she couldn't live a lie. She didn't love him.

Head down, she stepped from the shower and slid on Nick's robe. She had a towel wrapped around her head turban-style, and when she looked up, he grinned at her in the mirror. "Did I say good morning yet?" Ann asked, slipping her arms around his waist.

"Not properly."

As he turned, she pressed her mouth against the

strong column of his neck. For a long moment, she absorbed the scent of soap and shaving cream clinging to him. "We are going back to bed, aren't we?"

Gliding a hand over her hip, Nick brought his mouth closer to hers. "Now."

"Yes, now," she answered on a soft sigh, snatching the towel draped around his hips.

Bright late-morning sunlight poured into the kitchen when they finally reached it. Sipping coffee, Ann knelt with one knee on the window seat by the bay window and gazed out at the snowflakes dancing on the air, sticking to the limbs of the large willow in Nick's backyard. Behind her, he sang softly. *Aida* had garnered his attention this morning.

While everything symbolized peacefulness, the same turmoil she'd felt while showering plagued her. Today she had an appointment at four with Pablo. Stephanie had insisted he was the only one Gillian permitted to touch her hair. How snobbish that sounded. Perhaps that woman lingered inside her, but Ann couldn't identify with her. Tired of the emptiness that blocked her from herself, on a sigh, she whipped away from the window to join Nick at the stove. Peering over his shoulder, she watched him flip a pancake. "Do you know if the cat left?"

"You're still feeding him?"

"He's alone. You fed me when I was alone."

Nick transferred two pancakes to a plate and handed it to her, murmuring softly in her ear, "Not exactly the same."

Ann released a smoky laugh. "Sure it is."

To argue with her seemed futile. With her weight against him, he didn't want to think of possibilities. But one nagged at him. Possibly she wouldn't always be around, and the cat would still be meowing outside *his* door. Alley cats didn't belong in penthouse apartments or wherever.

"I only bought a few cans of cat food though," Ann assured him as she noticed the line deepening between his brows with his frown.

Nick focused on her. "Just don't bring him in," he said, not wanting the cat later as a constant reminder of her.

"He doesn't seem to want to come in."

At the airiness in her tone, Nick cracked a grin and lifted his hand from her waist. Obviously she'd tried to entice the cat. "The Count and I have an understanding."

Ann paused in pouring syrup over her pancakes. "Count?"

How had this conversation gotten started? Nick wondered. "*That* cat."

"Why Count?"

"Forget it."

Ann had learned she was relentless when curious. She waited until he settled on a kitchen chair, then eased around to the back of it, bent over and hooked her arms around his neck. "Why Count?" she whispered in his ear.

Oh, what the hell? She'd pester him until he told her. "Because before you started feeding him, like Dracula, he'd only come around at night."

Ann stroked his cheek before returning to her chair. Wisely she kept a straight face.

Head bent, Nick dug into breakfast. He'd never been a cat person. But this cat had played no coy games. He'd wanted food. He'd wanted petting. He'd wanted a home. Why the cat had chosen his house remained a mystery to Nick. Yesterday, he'd found it curled in a corner of the porch, using one of his boots for a pillow and declaring he'd chosen a home for himself.

So the man who'd shunned cats had one, the man who'd vowed to keep feet firmly planted where love was concerned had felt the earth move when a certain woman kissed him. And there was nothing he could do to change any of that. He'd succumbed to both woman and cat without much of a battle. Looking up, he saw her poking at breakfast. "What's happening here?" he asked, tracing the frown on her lips with a fingertip.

"I was thinking about the other night at my grandmother's. After dinner, she had a guest—the family doctor."

"Were you feeling ill?"

At the tinge of alarm in his voice, Ann smoothed a hand over the hair at the nape of his neck. "No, I wasn't. My grandmother insisted on a checkup. Of course, he said everything was okay." But the distinguished white-haired man had sent her grandmother a worried glance when Ann had started questioning him. "I thought he might be able to tell me something about my mother. Everyone else is so reluctant. And since the doctor has known my grandmother for years, he seemed like a worthy source for information."

"So you learned something else about her?" he asked, looking puzzled.

"He clarified a great deal. He told me my mother was high-strung. That she had difficulty coping with problems. Plain and simple, she battled mental illness most of her life, and died at a private hospital." Ann held back what she found most difficult repeating. He'd also told her that her mother had lost all touch with reality before she died.

"Not what you expected?"

"I didn't expect anything," Ann admitted softly. "I must have missed her. I feel sorrow not like a daughter would for a mother, but for the woman who suffered so much."

Nick kissed her temple. She was a woman of compassion and heart. Perhaps too much of both. Just as she'd love passionately, she'd be hurt deeply.

"Let's take a walk in the park," Ann said when finishing the last of her pancake, feeling eager for a little more time with him.

For minutes, in a comfortable silence, they walked across a field of snow. Ann wished she could keep moments like this forever. As she watched two youngsters romping in the snow, a sense of serenity washed over her. It couldn't last, she knew. She had problems, one major one named Redmond Harper. Pushing the toe of her boot into the fresh snow, she considered tonight's party. Rather than put herself on exhibit and reveal to all that she had no memory of anyone there, she'd play the role of Gillian Somerset.

But when, if ever, would she feel totally comfortable as that woman? she wondered.

Battling the wind, Nick slanted a sideways glance at her. Damp from the snow, her hair glistened, inviting his touch. "You're quiet."

Not wanting to spoil their time together, Ann grinned. "A rarity."

Lightly Nick traced the curve of her lips, hating to snatch the smile from her, but he had to ask. "Does the fiancé know I'm coming with you tonight?"

She needed no prompting that Redmond existed. She'd endured his touch when she'd craved Nick's. Since learning her identity, she'd felt the pressure of plans made by someone she didn't know—herself. "That won't be a problem." She hoped that would be the case, though she'd had to think quickly on her feet with excuses about too much to do beforehand to keep him from picking her up.

Nick still thought differently. "Ann—"

"There is no other man," she said, facing him. With gloved fingers, she caressed his jaw and traced a high cheekbone. "I'm not going to marry him."

Nick allowed himself a moment of joy. Only a moment. An abundance of common sense forced him to halt the beginnings of fantasies about marriage, kids, days together stretching into months and years. "What you feel now might change when you get your memory back."

Ann flattened herself against him. "You're saying I'll remember Redmond?"

"And what you felt for him."

Tugging off a glove, she slid her hand around his

cold neck. He expected her to forget him, to turn away. She rejected the idea as quickly as it formed. She'd never give up what they had.

With time to spare before her late-afternoon appointment at the hair salon, Ann urged Nick to stay with her while she stopped at a boutique near her apartment.

"Buying a dress for tonight?" Nick asked, eyeing a glittery one draped over a pinkish-colored chair. No price tag, he noted.

Since she had a closet overflowing with designer gowns, the thought of buying a new dress had never entered Ann's mind. "No, a present for Stephanie." She ended up purchasing a sweater, an Irish import, for her cousin, and a shawl for her grandmother. When she was waiting for the saleswoman to finish calculating the transaction, Ann fingered her hair. Ridiculously she felt nervous about her hair appointment. "I have to see the great Pablo." She rolled her eyes. "He sounds very formidable."

"Don't let him do anything wacky to this," Nick said softly while he caressed a strand.

"I won't." On a laugh, Ann looked down in unison with him. "You're beeping."

"I hate this thing." Nick read the phone number and frowned. "Be with you in a minute."

While he made the phone call, Ann ambled to the window of the boutique. A darkening gray sky promised more snow. Lunchtime traffic was heavy and cars stalled before reaching the Michigan Avenue Bridge.

Aware that Redmond's office was nearby, Ann de-

bated with herself about an impromptu stop. She
wanted him to understand her feelings. Marriage to
him seemed like something that was happening to
someone else. She couldn't recall the engagement, the
plans. They'd happened when she'd been obviously
caught up in her love for him. But now was different.
If only she could think of a way to save his pride and
ease out of the engagement.

"Here you are, Ms. Somerset," the saleswoman
said, handing Ann an elegant-looking bag with the
store's name embossed on it. "And thank you. Please
come again."

"I will," Ann answered, distracted by the view of
a flashy red sports car through the boutique window.
Behind the steering wheel, a sleek-looking brunette
with hair cut in a fashionable wedge leaned toward
her companion to kiss his cheek. Ann stared harder
at the blond man in the passenger seat. Redmond?
Was that him? If he would turn his face forward, she
could see his profile.

She dashed out the door, but traffic had surged forward. Visually she traced the car until it disappeared
from sight, heading away from the downtown area. If
it had been Redmond, he was going away from his
office, not toward it. She gave the woman little
thought. His cousin Trish had been a stranger. Everyone he knew, friend or family, were strangers to her.
What bothered her more were all the missed oppor-
tunities to end the lie she'd been living for days about
him. Sighing, she started to step back into the boutique when the door flew open.

"Come on," Nick said, and without an explanation, grabbed her hand to propel her toward the car.

Anxiety rose within Ann immediately. "What's wrong? Where are we going?"

"The hospital."

"Someone's hurt?"

Nick grinned widely. "My sister's having her baby."

Everyone was waiting when they dashed out of the hospital elevators. "How is she?" Nick asked, recalling how tired his sister had looked the other day when he'd stopped at the restaurant.

His mother met them. "Nothing's happened yet."

"She said her back hurt," his father announced to anyone who was listening.

"She should have stayed home today," Angelo, the papa-to-be, commented, running his hand over his bald head.

Ushering his mother back to a seat, Nick watched Ann moving to sit with Mara on one of the sofas. He liked seeing her this way. With her fairness, she looked pale in comparison to the rest of them. Yet she looked right being here with his family.

In passing, Nick patted Angelo's shoulder. "Babies come when they want. Remember when Jessie was born," he said about Mara's daughter. "None of us were around. Some guy we'd never met took her to the hospital."

With the recollection, everyone smiled in Rick's direction.

"Lucky me," Mara quipped, beaming back at her

husband, who was beside her, perched on the arm of the sofa.

Lovingly Rick touched her hair. "No. Lucky me."

More smiles circled the room.

Two hours later, no one was smiling or calm.

"How much longer?" Nick's father asked, pacing.

Angelo had disappeared into the labor room minutes ago.

Beside Ann, Nick's mother delivered a strained smile. "You've been busy?"

Ann didn't doubt the reason for Teresa's small talk. She was worried about her daughter. Maybe she worried for her son, too? He'd been hurt before badly. "Yes. I didn't have a chance to thank you for the recipe. It—"

Teresa's smile spread to her eyes. "Nick told me that it was delicious."

He'd said the same to her, but verification by someone else pleased her.

Crossing the room to her, for the umpteenth time, Nick checked the clock on the wall. As he settled beside Ann, he inclined his head close to hers. "It's past five," he said as a reminder. "You'd better leave. You're due at a party."

Her mind fixed on the happening around her, Ann presented him with a you've-got-to-be-kidding look. "You expect me to leave without knowing—" She cut her words short as Angelo materialized from the delivery room and half jogged to them.

"It's a boy! A boy," he yelled.

Within minutes, they'd gathered in the room with

Angelo, Bianca and their new son, Joseph. Happiness and love flowed around the room.

"He's got more hair than you," Nick teased the proud father, and accepted his new nephew in his arms.

Ann's heart tugged at the sight of Nick cradling the infant. He'd make a wonderful daddy. This tough man who gave free time to Little League, who saved silly trinkets, who possessed so much tenderness.

Gently she touched the baby's small hand, the tiny fingers. Was it maternal instincts that made her wish for a child of her own suddenly? Or was it a desire to give this man a baby, to share with him all the joy and wonderment of watching their child grow?

"Must come from the Vincetti side," Angelo quipped, and smoothed a hand over his bald head.

"Angelo thinks he looks like me," Bianca smiled brightly. "I say he looks like him."

"Who cares." Teresa stroked the soft dark tuft of her grandson's head. "He's beautiful and healthy."

At Nick's urging, Ann left for her apartment to get ready for the party. Draining the last of the thick vending-machine coffee, Nick waited for his brother-in-law before they headed back to Bianca's room.

"Mara told me that it's going to be a rough night for your lady." Rick tossed his paper cup into a receptacle. "A party. Lots of people. No memory of them."

Nick had been stalling from going home to shower and dress. If he didn't show tonight, he convinced himself he'd make life less difficult for her. He never doubted Ann could deal with tonight's festivities. While her confidence might be shaky, more than once she'd revealed a resilience and a strength of character many people didn't possess. But in a soul-searching moment, thanks to his brother-in-law, he admitted he hadn't been thinking of her feelings. He'd been protecting his own. His feelings be damned—hers should matter more. "Writers don't waste words," he commented, having read some of Rick's newspaper columns that had cut down politicians with swift quickness.

"We're known for that." Rick chuckled. "I have tickets for a hockey game next Thursday. Guy's night out."

Nick returned an amused smile. There had been a time not too long ago when Nick had invited his brother-in-law out for a similar evening. What existed between Rick and Mara had been shaky then. "Think I need one of those?"

"When you suggested it, I did. Not too long after, everything worked out okay for me. Could for you, too."

Could it? he wondered, looking down in response to his beeper. "Got to make a call."

Nick reached the nearest phone and punched the number for the squad room. The moment Riley started talking, he knew he had real trouble to deal with.

Chapter Twelve

Ann had left Nick with one goal in mind. To get her memory back now. In her apartment, instead of dressing for the party, she began in the kitchen, letting her fingers skim the stark white counter, the black coffeemaker. She supposed she'd never made coffee in this kitchen, since she hadn't known how, until she'd met Nick. She sensed she'd changed a lot from the woman who used to be waited on by a maid.

Moving through each room, she touched cordial glasses and vases, throw pillows, books, the surfaces of furniture. As if she were psychic, she tried to feel something, some attachment with the objects. She couldn't recall buying any of them, remember why a particular statue had caught her eye.

When she'd been at the hospital emergency room, the doctor had told her before she'd left that she couldn't force her memory back. She hated admitting that he'd been right.

With a glance at the clock, she swore, then rushed around to be ready on time. She was fastening an earring when Nick arrived. "I thought you'd chicken out," she said on a laugh while opening the door for him.

He smiled as she fell against him. The word *beautiful* failed to adequately describe her in a cranberry gown with long sleeves, a high neck and an enticing back that dipped to a low vee. The princess in the castle glowed with diamonds and sapphires twinkling at her ears. She looked stunning. "Only if you're willing," he finally answered.

"You're the one who told me I had to go," she reminded him, nibbling lightly at his ear.

He heard a recognizable sensuous sound in her voice. If he said the word, she wouldn't go. Knowing that forced only one answer from him. "Guess we go."

Through hooded lids, Ann met his stare. "Talk about no enthusiasm."

"I've been to parties like this before."

"Boring, huh?"

Nick chuckled. "Yeah."

"But—" Ann paused and raised her face to his. "You've never been to one with me before. And I'll make it up to you."

He feigned a put-upon look. "All right. I'll go. If—"

Ann tsked. "If? You have an if?"

"If you tie this," he said, flicking the tuxedo tie hanging at his collar.

"My pleasure." She smiled while her hands worked deftly at the task. "They are all going to be green with envy when I walk in with you."

Nick skimmed her hip in the velvet dress. He wished for the much softer texture of her skin. "You look beautiful."

Ann warmed with his words. "So do you."

Tilting his head, he released a muffled laugh against the side of her neck.

"Stand still. I'm almost done," she said on a giggle as his lips coursed down her neck and tickled her. "I'll never get this tied."

"That's the idea."

Despite his lighthearted mood at her apartment, Nick felt tension tightening the muscles in the back of his neck when the Somerset butler opened the door for them.

In the foyer, some blonde in a shimmering silver dress was droning on, "My first husband, no, my second, and I stayed at Auntie Cissy's summer cottage on Martha's Vineyard. We simply love it there."

How had he managed to come full circle? Nick wondered. The woman nearby possessed the same aloofness in her expression as the women Ann had had lunch with, as Julia often had. In fairness, he'd admit he liked Sara, mostly because he'd sensed a genuine warmth from her for Ann. The other two women Ann had been with were another matter. Ann's cousin was shallow and slightly lightweight in the brains department. The third woman, Redmond's cousin, he'd never met, but Nick had seen her scan his family's restaurant with disdain.

Easing his hand from Ann's, he set it at her back. With the slight pressure near her shoulder blades, she cast a look up at him. Once again, he thought she looked breathtaking. And vulnerable. She'd hid her nervousness well, but he'd felt it earlier in the hand that had death-gripped his.

During the drive, he'd debated about relaying what Riley had told him. For the first time since she'd entered his life, he possessed knowledge that he'd kept from her. That didn't sit well with him, but he kept wondering if she didn't have enough to deal with tonight. "Go in." He gave her waist a squeeze and stepped back, alert to the predicament he'd generate if he stayed too close to her. "They're expecting you," he said about the guests wandering into the ballroom toward the soft tones of a piano and the music of Gershwin.

Uneasiness skittering through her, Ann drew a deep breath, the kind meant to calm anxiousness. "Stay near," she whispered before gliding away.

Immediately she found herself in the midst of strangers and in position between her grandmother and Redmond to greet guests. She performed as expected—smiling, pretending to people who knew nothing about her memory loss. But repeatedly she agonized over her deceitfulness as she nodded in response to good wishes about the forthcoming wedding, to remarks about her and Redmond being a per-

fect match. And she knew the time had come to stop
this.

She couldn't pretend any longer. She wasn't sure
if Nick loved her, but she knew that she wasn't in
love with Redmond. For some reason, she felt she
never would be.

Working her way through groups, she made eye
contact with Nick before sidling close to him. "I wish
we were somewhere else," she said, reaching for the
glass in his hand. She took a sip of the Scotch. What
she longed for was to be alone with him.

His collar tight, Nick managed not to squirm. "It's
comforting to know that you've been as miserable as
me."

Handing him back his glass, Ann smiled up at him,
then slipped her hand in his. It was the first genuine
smile she'd felt since they'd arrived, and it was because of him. As more people filled the room, she felt
almost claustrophobic. She fingered the skirt of her
gown while she suppressed nervousness. She wanted
to step outside, stare into one man's face, not a room-
ful of strangers. "We could sneak away," she said,
discreetly pushing her hip against his.

With the movement of her head, the diamonds at
her ear winked at him. "Too late. We've been spotted."

Tracing his stare, Ann wrinkled her nose as she saw
Redmond weaving his way to them and glaring at
Nick.

For Ann's sake, Nick unlaced his fingers from hers.
"See you later," he said, and eased away.

Ann wanted to stop him; she didn't, aware Felicia

might suffer embarrassment if male tempers flared over her granddaughter.

"Why is that detective here?" Redmond asked as he approached.

"I invited him." Why did she always want to draw away from this man? Ann wondered. Why hadn't her feelings for him ever warmed like they had with her grandmother, with Sara, with Stephanie? This was crazy. She was being unfair to him and dishonest. She needed to have a necessary heart-to-heart talk with him about them. She'd been like some ostrich hiding her head in the sand, not acknowledging a future planned before her amnesia. She couldn't go on ignoring it, not now, not when she was in love with Nick. "Redmond, we need to talk." It wasn't the best place, but she couldn't go on with the charade.

With the glass of Scotch in his hand, Nick wandered through the French doors that led from the ballroom onto a terrace. Wintry air tossed his hair. Light and unhurried snowflakes fluttered down beyond the covered terrace.

"You're not enjoying yourself?"

He pivoted in response to the voice of Ann's grandmother. "It's cold out here, Mrs. Somerset."

Slowly her wheelchair inched closer to him. "Yes, it's fortunate I wore my shawl. You didn't answer my question."

Nick had met hordes of Julia's relatives and disliked most of them. He couldn't say the same about this woman. Not only wisdom but also humor flashed often in her intelligent eyes. "I'm here because your granddaughter requested that I come."

"I didn't think you were a party crasher." Her eyes danced with humor. "Isn't that what they call people who do that?"

He'd never gone anywhere he wasn't welcomed. "That's what they call them."

"In my day, they were simply referred to as riff-raff."

Nick maintained a fixed, unemotional expression. Was there a message for him in her words?

She laughed so softly it was barely audible. "My husband's father was considered riffraff. My husband, too. Did you know that Gillian's great-great-grandfather worked as a bookbinder in his youth? A hardworking man. He was never afraid of getting his hands dirty. In time, he worked his way up the success ladder, and he was eventually able to buy a publishing house. Still he wasn't immediately accepted into society. Too common, by their standards. Despite the family's success, my father threatened to call the authorities if Jonathan, my late husband, didn't leave me alone." A stronger laugh, a musical sound, filled the air. "Jonathan worked hard until my father couldn't ignore him, then announced that with him I would have everything my father could give me."

Never could he make that promise.

Briefly her gaze shifted to the terrace doors and the party beyond them. "You'll have to excuse an old woman, but reminiscing about those days is such a joy for me. Such a strong and handsome and gentle man he was." Love warmed her voice. "It's easy for a woman to love a man like that. To my pleasure, my granddaughter takes after me. We don't like others to tell us what to do. We like to make our own decisions about everything, including the men we welcome into our lives.'' She pressed a button and moved her chair toward the doors that led into the house. ''I won't ask if you love her,'' she said, stopping at the opened French doors. ''I can see you do when you look at her.''

''Mrs. Somerset—'' Nick waited until she looked back at him. ''I have some information that I need to tell you.''

Inside, Ann skirted two couples in an intense discussion about local politics. From across the room, her grandmother wheeled in from the terrace and signaled to her. Keeping a smile in place, Ann breezed her way past couples, acknowledging comments in passing before reaching her.

''It's quite warm in here, isn't it?'' Felicia spoke low. ''Fortunately, I had company when I was outside. You might like to step onto the terrace for a minute or two.''

The message delivered came through clearly. Ann squeezed her grandmother's hand, then opened the terrace door. She found Nick standing near a birdbath statue. It and the pond had been drained for winter. ''Can I escape with you?'' she asked, unsure of his mood.

A grin, a simple grin from him, soothed her. ''You're going to be cold.''

Bridging the space between them, she took his hands. "Will I be?"

With her good-humored tease, Nick slid an arm around her waist and tugged her closer until her soft contours felt as one with him. Heat radiated through him. He hadn't realized until that moment how much he'd needed the contact with her.

Ann draped a hand over his shoulder. "Dance with me."

In the shadowy light, she was enveloped in a pale, soft glow. As her hair flowed back from her face beneath the cold wind, he caught the silky strands. "I hope you're not expecting great," Nick murmured in her ear when he gathered her close.

As they swayed, she smiled. "You're wonderful." In more ways than she'd ever told him. For a few moments, she let the music float over her while she relaxed against him. In his arms, she didn't feel the cold. In his arms, she escaped from the troubles so close at hand. For a little while, even if for only seconds, it was wonderful to dance beneath moonlight, to forget everything and everyone else. She knew that wouldn't last, couldn't. Too much weighed heavily on her mind.

"You're too quiet," Nick observed quietly.

So easily he read her. "Am I such an open book to you now?" she asked on a strained laugh. He kept staring at her as if trying to see what wasn't visible, and she gave up trying to hide her true feelings. After all, she sought him out, because of all the people she could have talked to, he was the one she'd felt comfortable revealing her most private thoughts to; he was the one she trusted most.

Feather light, Nick touched the faint line etched between her brows. "What are you worrying about? Did it go badly with Harper?"

Ann spoke her concern. "I've been trying not to hurt anyone."

"You can't always do that," he said softly, touching her hair, wondering when would be the last time.

"But I want to. I don't want to be responsible for someone else's pain."

Nick cupped the back of her neck and pressed her cheek against his. He'd seen her deep caring for others repeatedly. He'd seen it with his family when she moved from one family member to another with optimistic comments during the wait at the hospital. He'd seen the same caring with the cat that she couldn't turn away.

"I am though." Ann reluctantly drew back. "I told him. I told Redmond that it's over."

Nick wondered if his heart had stopped. "You broke the engagement?"

Wrapped in his embrace, she wanted to see his eyes, hoping that within them was the love she was yearning for. "Yes," she whispered, because to say it louder seemed wrong.

Nick needed a second to think. Was she saying that she wanted to be with him? Had she made a choice between them? Or was this simply a decision because she felt nothing for Harper? "You told me what you said." Nick fought his own insecurities. "What did he say?"

Her chin raised in that defiant manner he'd seen often enough when she was enduring a battle within herself. "He won't give up. He believes I'm confused."

That was possible, Nick knew. That was what had bothered him since he'd first admitted to himself that he loved her.

"I suppose I should go in," she said softly, tempted to share what was in her heart for him. "Give me five minutes."

Not fast enough, Nick thought. Tenderly he stroked her cheek with a callused finger while the fingers of his other hand wound into her hair. At a pleasurable, languid pace, he took a fill of her taste. "Five minutes," he said before releasing her.

Just in time to avoid a scene.

Smiling from his insistence, Ann turned, then stilled in midstride at the sight of Redmond standing in the shadowed light between the brightness of the party and the darkness outside.

"Here you are. People are asking for you."

Ann traced his annoyed glare to Nick.

"And your grandmother was looking for you."

Since her grandmother had suggested she step outside, Ann knew for a fact that was a lie. Returning a steady stare, she joined him at the door. For a few minutes more, she'd do what was expected. But only for a few more minutes.

A step ahead of Redmond, Ann steered them toward friends of hers.

As she'd hoped, Trish rushed to her. "Come with me. You must see the woman Trey Belmont brought,'' she whispered out of the corner of her mouth. ''For one itsy-bitsy moment, Redmond,'' she insisted as she noticed his scowl.

Willingly Ann let herself be led by Trish. ''That was an excuse,'' Trish said over her shoulder with a laugh the moment they were away from Redmond. ''Taylor and Sabrina want to know about your policeman.''

Expectant and curious expressions met her as Trish steered her toward two other women. Strangers, Ann reflected. More strangers. She smiled and fielded the questions about Nick as noncommittally as she could, then begged a need for the rest room.

What she really needed was to get on with her life. She couldn't pretend nothing had changed. She was a different woman from the one who'd agreed to wed Redmond. It was time to stop beating herself up because she couldn't be the person everyone remembered.

Approaching two women deep in conversation, she zigzagged to the left to step around a pillar and avoid bothering them.

''Did you see her?'' the one woman was saying in a stage whisper to her companion.

Eavesdropping seemed rude, but Ann halted, stunned at the other woman's response.

''I can't believe Redmond invited her. And that dress. Purple is so garish.''

''I heard Gillian doesn't remember,'' she said in a conspiratorially low voice. ''Can you imagine?''

The first woman released an amused short laugh,

totally unaware Ann was in earshot. "If that's true he probably assumed she'd never know who Paula was."

Before she'd finished talking, Ann was surveying the room of dancing couples for a woman in a purple dress. She wasn't hard to find. Standing near the buffet table, a tall brunette had captured the attention of several males. Ann wound her way to Stephanie, not feet from the gathered group. "Who is that?" Ann asked softly.

Her mouth full, Stephanie paused in reaching for another lobster-stuffed mushroom. "Who?" she mumbled.

Ann touched her shoulders and angled her in the brunette's direction. "Her."

Her eyes widening, Stephanie took an excruciatingly lengthy time to finish chewing the food in her mouth.

Ann gripped her arm firmly. "Who is she?" she asked, assuring her cousin she wasn't letting go until she got an answer.

"Paula VanGleson. She's from a nouveau riche family that isn't doing well."

Ann wanted to know one more thing. "And who is she to Redmond?"

Stephanie's shoulders sagged. "Gilly," she whined, acting as if she were being tortured.

Ann ignored her pleading look. "Answer me."

"She's Redmond's ex-fiancée."

"Ex?" Was she really? Ann wondered, taking a step away. She knew now she had seen Redmond with the same woman in the flashy red sports car earlier. Weaving a path around people, Ann cornered him. She needed to ask a few questions of her own.

In the foyer, Nick draped Ann's coat over his arm and slouched against a wall. Conversation and sporadic subdued laughter drifted to him, reminding him of similar endless parties he'd attended with Julia.

Julia. Why was he remembering the time with her? The last night they were together she'd ripped him open. He would never forget her departing words, ones he'd never told anyone. "I never loved you." He'd been numb, not believing her, not wanting to accept the truth about his marriage. He'd been made a fool.

But was he being one again? He'd told Ann not to be a victim of her own fear. Was he letting his pride make him one, stopping him from taking another chance with a woman who'd shown him nothing except love?

In response to the sound of footsteps, he pushed away from the wall. As Ann strolled toward him, he met her halfway. So much had changed since their last conversation. Mostly he'd stopped being stupid. He wanted to say words of love. He wanted to shout them. Instead he kept them to himself. She looked pale. As he held her coat and she slipped into it, he felt her tension. "Did Harper do something?"

Ann decided that might definitely be an understatement. "I'm beginning to wonder if I can believe anything anyone says. I keep looking for honesty. Am I expecting too much?" she asked in a tone that was weighed down with disgust.

Nick curled his fingers over her shoulders. "Tell me what he did."

"Not here," Ann insisted, conscious they'd become the center of attention for several departing guests. She braved speculative stares. No doubt she'd be *the* name on the tongues of morning gossipers.

Nick waited only until they were settled in his car. "Now tell me."

She sighed while she gathered her thoughts. Raking gloved fingers through her wind-tossed hair, she stared at the dark dashboard while she relayed the overheard conversation about Paula VanGleson and Redmond. "I thought at first that Stephanie might be lying, but when I asked Redmond about her, he insisted she was only an acquaintance. I didn't tell him what I'd heard, but why would he pretend he hardly knew her? Because he had something to hide? Or to protect me? I'd already told him I wasn't going to marry him. News about him and another woman would have hardly broken my heart. All I wanted was the truth."

Truth could haunt a person. Frowning, Nick peered past windshield wipers laboring to push snow away as he negotiated a turn off the private driveway and onto the highway. With the weather meriting his full attention, he wished now he hadn't started driving. Headlights dimmed by a slanting sheet of snow beamed a narrow tunnel on the highway. To shield her, he'd held back what Riley had told him, reasoning that learning the truth had to be less upsetting than having it told to her, but he wondered if his own arrogance would smack him down. He knew how she felt about honesty. He kept his eyes on traffic as he admitted, "He's been seeing her."

At first Ann thought she misunderstood him. "What did you say?"

Nick cursed as a passing car cut sharply in front of them on the slick street, jockeying between their car and another one. "I've been checking on him. I learned he has a second apartment, one occupied by Paula VanGleson." Peripherally he saw her shake her head, as if muddled and trying to grasp some rational thought.

"You knew and didn't tell me?" Repeatedly she'd agonized, not wanting to hurt Redmond, but had known she had to break the engagement. "How could you not tell me?"

The accusation in her voice ripped through him.

"I trusted you. How long...? Nick!"

The alarm that jumped in her voice equaled the tension in him. Ahead of them, the same car swept out for another pass. Fishtailing, it barely missed the rear bumper of one car.

In horror, Ann watched it skid across the other lane of traffic, then slam into the highway guardrail. Cars veered away to dodge the crash. Gasping, she gripped the armrest as the headlights of an oncoming car aimed straight for them.

"Hang on." Nick cut hard toward the highway shoulder.

Jerked forward and to the side, Ann bumped her head against the door. The jolt seemed inconsequential. Behind them, the tires of other cars squealed. Everything seemed to happen in slow motion. Terror clutching her, she hung on to the door's armrest with a white-knuckled grip while they took a jostling ride over the rough surface. Beside her, Nick cursed. More seconds passed, one after another with agonizing slowness, before he brought the car to a skidding stop. Trembling, she fought not to sob.

"Ann!"

Gently she felt the touch of Nick's hand on her shoulder. "I'm all right. Just shaky." Through the gauzy haze of the snowstorm, she saw headlights beaming in odd directions from the road. "That was awful," she said unsteadily, still trembling.

Nick stroked her cheek softly. His gut untightened from the fear that had nearly controlled him because she'd sat so still for a few seconds. Heaving several calming breaths, he squinted at the bedlam on the highway. "I have to see if I can help." He shoved open the door. With the dome light on, he offered himself a quick assurance. Though she shuddered, she appeared uninjured. "Use the cellular. Call emergency."

At the slam of the door, Ann shook her head slightly, trying to clear her mind, and fumbled for the cellular phone. She punched out the number for emergency. Snow veiled the outline of the car smashed against the rail. When the call was finished, she started to move, to open the door, wanting to help. Her body refused the message from her brain.

Her head spun with images, memories. A multitude of emotions swarmed her. She wanted to run from them and couldn't. Shutting her eyes, she remembered everything. Everything. With clarity, she watched herself on that rainy night weeks ago.

She'd been at her grandmother's home, descending the winding staircase. The clock had struck eight right before the phone had rung. She'd listened to the caller, shock numbing her, then she'd grabbed her purse and a jacket. She recalled throwing them into the back of her car. She remembered later, clutching one key, dashing into a building, riding an elevator. She'd opened a door, moved quietly. Why quietly? Because she'd heard voices.

In the distance, the sound of sirens intruded. Ann snapped open her eyes. On the highway before her, she saw a flash of red, then another as emergency vehicles arrived. Nick was bathed in the glow of one red light, talking to a uniformed officer.

The scene before her gave way to another. Not what she'd seen but what she'd heard had rocked her that rainy night weeks ago. She remembered running from the voices. The rain beating at her face when she'd dashed back to her car. The hum of the engine. Driving with no destination in mind. She'd wanted to be alone, to think. The weather had worsened. She hadn't known where she was. At some moment, she'd driven off the main highway not caring where she was going.

"Ann."

The sound of Nick's voice and the sudden sweep of cold damp air brought her back to the present.

For the second time in minutes, fear for her pounced on him. The dark interior of the car shadowed her face, preventing him from seeing her eyes clearly, but she looked paler. Too pale. "What's wrong?"

"I remember," Ann managed to utter. "I must have been driving too fast, lost control of the car, and it went off the road." She drew a shuddery breath. "I remember fighting my way through brush, struggling to my feet, falling." She grappled for words though the images played clearly in her mind. "That must be when I hit my head."

Nick caught her shoulders, wanting to hold her, and felt her tremble. "You know why you were there?"

No, she didn't, not really. She knew only why she'd been driving. She hadn't thought about where she was or where she'd been headed.

At a rapping on his window, Nick tossed a deadly look at a uniformed cop who appeared barely old enough to shave.

"We need your statement," he said when Nick rolled down the window.

"In a minute," Nick insisted.

Ann noted the policeman's indecisiveness. "Detective, could you come now?" he asked.

"Dammit, no!" Nick yelled. "Ann, we have to talk."

She shook her head as if trying to block his words and grabbed the cellular phone again. "I have to go to my grandmother's."

"Take my car, and I'll meet you there."

Unsteady, she didn't want to drive. "I'll get a cab."

Again the uniformed officer rapped on the window. As first cop on the accident scene, Nick had no choice. He had to stay and make a statement. "I want to know what happened," he said, opening the car door.

"Don't you know everything already?"

Slowly, maybe because he was afraid of what he'd see in her eyes, his gaze came back to her. The warmth was gone from her eyes. "I told you what I know."

"Did you?" she asked, distrust thick in her tone. She wanted to believe him, but he'd broken a promise to her. "So you say now, but you didn't tell me about Redmond and Paula." How could she know if he hadn't learned more and kept that from her, too?

Nick wanted to defend himself. There wasn't time. Bowing his head from an onslaught of snowflakes, he trudged toward the smashed car and emergency vehicles. Over his shoulder, he saw her on the phone in his car. More than distance was separating them.

Chapter Thirteen

Ann made two phone calls, one of them to Redmond. Behind her, stuck in traffic, a cab answered her second call, whizzing along the shoulder of the road to Nick's car to pick her up, then U-turned toward the suburbs. Because the driver visualized himself as an Indy 500 driver, she reached her grandmother's home before Redmond. It amazed her that she could feel so sad, yet when she dropped to her knees before Felicia's wheelchair, an inner joy warmed her. All the feelings she'd once known for her grandmother surged through her.

"My dear, I didn't expect you back."

"I've missed you, Grandma," Ann said with the affection that had evolved between them through the years.

The name jerked Felicia back. Searchingly her eyes

widened, then filled with comprehension and tears. "Oh! When?" she asked, her voice cracking.

"Minutes ago, I remembered everything," Ann informed her, blinking back her own tears as her grandmother gathered her close again. "I've asked Redmond to come back here. I wasn't certain if the party would be over."

"Almost immediately after you left."

Her wrinkled hands framing Ann's face, her grandmother regarded her. "Tell me now what happened to you."

Nick didn't give a damn if he was the last person Ann wanted to see. He'd been with her through all the days of unanswered questions. Even if she was through with him, he couldn't walk away. This was unfinished business.

When the butler opened the door, Nick strode past him, not intending on being stalled in the foyer. Hearing voices in the library, he sliced a hand in the air to put Charles off. "I'm going in."

The butler gave him a clear path. "Yes, sir."

Before Nick hit the arched doorway, he heard the sound of Redmond's voice raising excitedly.

"I'm so glad to hear this. I knew when you called you'd come to your senses. Now you say you remember everything?"

Some sense within Ann made her look away, certain Nick was near. Staying at a distance, he played spectator. She'd counted on his honesty. He'd promised it and then he'd... A different kind of hurt fluttered inside her. At the moment, she had no time to deal with it.

Redmond rounded a hard, resentful glare at Nick, then insisted on her attention. "When did that happen?"

"Unexpectedly after leaving. I know why I called my grandmother and told her I was going on a trip with Sara." Ann fixed a stare on him. "Because of you."

"Me?" He released a mirthless laugh. "You have everything mixed up. I didn't even see you that evening."

"Yes, but I saw you. I used the key you had given me for your apartment. I needed to talk to you."

He stared unseeingly, as if caught up in a scene in his mind. "But you didn't." He turned puzzled eyes on her. "What did you want to talk to me about?"

"A phone call. I'm fortunate that people who work for my family are also friends. My grandmother's lawyer knows many insurance agents. The name Somerset doesn't go unnoticed. After her lawyer received a phone call from an acquaintance, he immediately called and informed me that you were interested in a hefty insurance policy on me. Interesting," she said as an old fury baited her.

Bracing a shoulder against the wall, Nick took extreme pleasure in watching the man suddenly squirm.

"There's some misunderstanding," Redmond insisted. "Did he mention I also requested one for myself?"

He was smooth. But not quite good enough, Ann

reflected. She'd had the presence of mind to ask the lawyer that very question. "No, you didn't."

"Felicia, she's confused, of course, because of the amnesia," he appealed to her grandmother.

"Is she? I think what she's saying is rather enlightening."

Looking uncertain, he whipped back to Ann. "You aren't yourself."

Ann swung away, feeling ire sapping the strength from her legs, and leaned against the arm of a settee. "After the phone call, I went to your apartment to confront you about it, and guess what? You were busy, very busy in *bed* with Paula."

At the anger in her voice, Nick stepped closer to see her face. What she was saying didn't make sense to him. He'd gotten to know a woman who seemed like more of a fighter than a runner. He'd held back information about Redmond because of the party, but he'd planned to tell her. He'd thought she'd be upset, but he never imagined that if she'd seen her fiancé in bed with another woman, she'd fly from the house, or that it would cause her amnesia. There had to be more, Nick decided.

"Gillian, I can explain." Despite a winter tan, Redmond blanched.

So had Ann, Nick noted. He'd like to stop her. There was too much pain in her eyes. What had she remembered that had devastated her so much?

"It was a moment of weakness," Redmond said with an appealing look. "Paula has been after me all the time we were engaged but I—"

"Don't, Redmond." By her fingertips, she hung on

to her composure. "Your lies won't work anymore. Try them on someone more gullible. I'm not that person now. Frankly I'm grateful I was saved from seeing you two in a clinch. You were busy talking. I heard your plan. You laughed because you'd already persuaded me to marry you sooner. What a chore it would be to keep pretending. But you assured her it wouldn't take long. Once you married me, the money would be easier for you to get. That's what you promised her. Then you'd take over everything I own."

He sputtered out a denial. "I wouldn't say that. You misunderstood. I love you."

"Oh, please," Ann said with disgust. "I heard you." She allowed the coldness she felt to enter her voice. "With my mother's past, people wouldn't require much convincing that mental illness had been inherited. As a loving husband, you could see that I was hospitalized. Then you could appeal to the courts to designate you to handle the estate. All you needed was a little time to make me believe I wasn't mentally stable." Ann swallowed hard to battle the uneasiness in her stomach. "Prove me crazy. That was your little plan."

Redmond held out his arms, palms up. "Gillian, I don't know why you're saying this. Perhaps, you believed you heard this, but—"

As she straightened her back, Nick could almost see the strength in her emerging.

"Get out," Ann said with as much calm as she could muster. "Your perfect little plan failed."

"Gillian, this is incredible. But, of course, you've been ill. When you come to your senses—"

Nick considered slugging Redmond.

"Are you deaf?" Ann flared. "I know your plan."
She had no use for him. She didn't even want to look
at him anymore. "Get out."

As if sensing defeat, he raised his chin. "This is
all a gross misunderstanding," he said, more to
Felicia in the manner of someone aware of the woman's power. "But clearly the engagement is off. I
could hardly marry your granddaughter now." Again
he gave Ann his attention. "You'll return the engagement ring, I assume."

For the second time in seconds, Nick wanted to
lower the man's nose a couple of inches.

Ann nearly laughed at the trace of haughtiness in
Redmond's voice. "Find it yourself. I flung it into a
Wisconsin river," she answered, turning her back on
him. She was still wrestling with anger when she
heard the front door slam.

"A scoundrel," her grandmother quipped. "In my
day, he'd have been run out of town."

To quiet her nerves, Ann took a deep breath before
facing her grandmother. She'd had clues. Sara's comment to Trish about the Harpers having no money,
just lineage. Redmond constantly preying on her absence of memory with words about her being confused. A brunette with him in a flashy sports car.

"I'm not surprised you didn't confront him," her
grandmother admitted, securing Ann's attention. "It
was your way to veil emotions. If someone did something against you, you hid your true feelings until
you'd determined how to handle the situation."

Yes, she had, Ann recalled. She'd become so mistrustful that she'd begun to doubt her own feelings, so she never acted impulsively. Dropping to a chair, she touched her head. It hurt again with too many images. "After hearing them, I left. I remember wanting to block the pain. It was with me again, the same sadness and blinding anger that I'd felt after Mark." Like him, Redmond had cared more about her money than her. The memories were back, not only of that night, but some that she'd blocked for years, and with them, so came the distrust she'd harbored since childhood.

She felt so betrayed again. Deceived. Foolish. She swallowed hard with a stunning realization. The emotions were flooding her as if weeks hadn't passed since that night. The pain, the humiliation, threatened to consume her. "He lied about everything." Curling her fingers into her palms, Ann released a despairing moan. "I wonder why I never saw him clearly before."

"Oh, my dear, I'm sure you did." Her grandmother's wheelchair moved, drawing Ann's attention to her. "You wanted a prenuptial agreement drawn up."

Nodding, Ann recalled the call from her lawyer several weeks before her amnesia. Redmond had missed his appointment to sign papers. "Yes, I had doubts about him before, too. What I don't understand is why I ever wanted to marry him."

"Gillian, he was very charming when he wanted to be," her grandmother assured her.

She recalled descriptions about him being smooth and shrewd. Deceitful, Ann had thought. "I wonder how long he'd planned this. From the beginning? So much makes sense now," she said, speaking thoughts. "Redmond knew about Mark, knew he'd only been attracted to me for my money. He knew of my disappointment with my father. He knew my mother's history with mental illness. I was an easy mark for him to use all that to his advantage." She remembered the voices again, the words now. *"It won't be difficult to make everyone believe her daughter's just as deranged as she was,"* Redmond had told Paula.

Ann ambled to the window. Snow fell with more authority. Freezing temperatures had coated branches of trees with sparkling icicles. A chill swept over her. "I remember driving, trying to understand Redmond's thinking, wondering if he was going to announce his affair or slowly let me discover it? Then he'd deny everything, convince others that I was the angry, distraught daughter of a woman who'd also had a history of jealousy and obsessive behavior. All he had to do was play the charming, loving husband who'd done everything he could for his wife, but she was slowly going insane, just like her mother," she said, unable to keep the hurt and bitterness out of her voice.

"He will pay," Felicia murmured in a soft and deadly tone. "I have a great deal of influence. I'm going to make sure people know he's a man who can't be trusted."

She'll protect me, Ann thought. No one would know what Redmond had planned, yet her grandmother would make sure his reputation was sullied.

"This has been entirely too long a day for me,"

her grandmother announced. "Are you all right, my dear?"

Putting on a brave front, Ann whipped to a stand with her best smile and bent over to hug Felicia. "You sleep well," she said, kissing her grandmother's velvety cheek.

"You, too, my dear. Good night, Nicholas."

Nick dragged his gaze from Ann to nod at her grandmother. "Good night, Mrs. Somerset." Now that he was alone with Ann, he wished for the right words. "It's been a difficult night," he said slowly, watching her. As she had the first night, she smoothed her thumb across her bare ring finger. Was she regretting the love lost? She'd felt anger at Redmond, but she must also have remembered love. After his divorce, Nick recalled he'd bounced between the two deep emotions for a long time. Aching for her, he stepped closer and caught the back of her neck. "It hurts a hell of a lot, doesn't it?" When she didn't resist his touch, he gathered her close.

A log snapped in the nearby fireplace. Ann looked at the flames dancing, the sparks spraying upward. Her mouth felt dry, her stomach unsettled. Mostly her mind was cluttered.

"I know you're angry at me. I'd planned to tell you." Nick could give her nothing, but excuses. How many other people had done that? "Are you holding it against me because I didn't tell you?"

"No," she answered, but she didn't feel as sure of him as she had before. Trust, she reflected. An intangible. For her something that seemed unobtainable, too. She realized in that instant that there had been comfort in not knowing. Now, with every breath she drew, she revisited all the times she'd been disillusioned by someone she loved. Her father, Mark, Redmond. This was the third time she'd believed a man's lies.

Gently Nick touched her chin, angling it up, needing to see her eyes. He spoke the words in his heart even as he suddenly wondered if she would believe him. "I know this is lousy timing, but you need to know it. I need to say it. I love you. I want to be with you."

Those were words Ann had yearned to hear from him before. She really wanted to believe in him, to believe what they'd shared was real. She loved him, too. She did. She thought she did. How could she know for sure? She'd made so many mistakes before. Other men had said those same words to her, and she'd believed them. They'd lied. Because the feel of Nick's arms around her only confused her more, she pulled free of them. She couldn't help the doubts building within her.

When she turned away, Nick needed a moment to catch his breath. This wasn't how he'd imagined this moment. Inclining his head to see her face more clearly, he tried to measure her mood. Cold, distant. He felt as if a different woman stood before him. An ache rising within him, he wanted to bridge the distance between them. He wanted to back up. Just for a few hours to when he was holding her, to when nothing was clear except the love he felt from her.

As he touched her shoulder, she stiffened. How had it come to this? He'd prepared for the end because of her love for another man. With Redmond out of the picture, everything should be all right between them. She'd regained her memory. She was free of commitments, and he was still losing her.

Ann kept her back to him. So much had happened. "Redmond claimed he loved me, too. Now I don't know if I can…" The words on the tip of her tongue seemed so unfair, but she couldn't help how she felt. She knew who she was. She should know, too, what she wanted, but she didn't.

"Finish it," Nick demanded.

Facing him, Ann wasn't sure of anything anymore except an old fear. He'd said he loved her. Trust and love went together, didn't they? Others had said they loved her; they hadn't. Could she believe him? Could she believe anyone? "I don't know who to trust."

She delivered a harder punch than he'd anticipated. What reasoning would help? Nick wondered, feeling desperate for the right words. "I'm not Redmond. I'm not that other guy."

Uncertainty plaguing her, Ann labored for a breath. Oh, how she wanted to believe in him.

"Say something."

"I don't know."

Nick couldn't back off; it wasn't his way. "You don't know what? If you love me?"

She squeezed her eyes shut for a second, trying to forget he'd broken a promise to her.

"Answer me." Frustration weaved through him at his own inadequacy to reach her. "What do you feel?"

She had doubts about him now. "Are you different from the others?"

Nothing else she might have said could have sliced through him so effectively. He saw tears in her eyes. He didn't even know what was causing them. "Dammit, if you love, you trust."

Exhausted, Ann turned away. "I've tried that before."

He stood for a moment, simply staring after her. "Not with me."

Not with me. His words echoed in her mind as she stood in the silence of the empty ballroom. Tears flowed, ones she'd never let free that night. Time hadn't helped her forget the evening she'd learned of Redmond's duplicity. The same agony when her pride, her self-worth, her trust were shattered bore down on her as if those moments had happened yesterday.

She wept for then, and now. Within her grasp had been happiness with Nick. She wanted him to be here, so why had she pushed him away? She loved him; she needed him. He was the last person she'd wanted to hurt.

Loneliness penetrated her. Was this what she'd searched for since losing her memory? Miserable, she leaned against a wall and closed her eyes. With each recollection, the emotion accompanying it returned. Pity for a mother she'd last seen rocking in a chair and staring with distant eyes out a window. Sadness and regret for a father who'd disappointed her repeatedly. Self-pity and youthful shame when she'd accepted that the first man she'd loved had measured her by how much she'd been worth.

Sighing, she opened her eyes with the memory of a happy day. Her ninth birthday party—laughing friends, streamers stretched beneath a white canopy, her father and grandmother smiling as she opened gifts. She'd had special moments. A debutante ball—a tall, young man looking at her as if she were beautiful. She'd felt beautiful in her white dress. Christmas—a favorite ornament of hers, a red bird that clipped on a branch.

"Gillian, you're still here?"

With fingertips, Ann brushed at moisture on her cheeks as her grandmother stopped her wheelchair in the arched doorway. "I thought you'd gone to bed."

"After parties, I sometimes—"

"Talk to Charles late at night," Ann finished for her, remembering now that her grandmother had always sought out the butler after guests had left. Long-time employees became old friends. He was one of those.

"I'd like to stay here tonight," Ann said, and prayed her grandmother didn't ask for an explanation.

Briefly a quizzical look flashed in her grandmother's eyes. If she had questions, she refrained from asking them. "You know you can. We can talk in the morning."

Unsteady, Ann moved forward. "Thank you."

Her grandmother hesitated a moment. "Nicholas is gone?"

Gone. Ann's gaze cut back to her. "Yes. He's gone."

* * *

With his car window open and the cold morning
air biting at his face, Nick drove along the lake on
his way home. Since leaving her, he'd repeatedly see-
sawed from anger to frustration to hurt and back to
anger.

Too keyed up to sleep, he'd detoured toward the
precinct last night. Typical behavior for a cop. Whenever snags occurred in their personal lives, they
buried themselves in their work. The distraction had
helped for a few hours, but as dawn had cast its dim
slanting light across desks in the squad room, he still
was weighed down with guilt. He'd promised himself
he wouldn't hurt her, and because of his own stupid-
ity, he'd made her believe he was no better than the
others.

Hell, she'd hurt him, too, though. He'd thought she
loved him. Had that been his own fault? Had he
fooled himself, drifted on some fantasy with a woman
named Ann, then when Gillian Somerset had entered
his life, he'd stupidly still believed in them? How
many times had he warned himself that whatever he
felt for her had no future? He'd forgotten that warning
as love had grown for her. So here he was again.

None of her sadness had abated by morning. In the
dining room, Ann sagged onto one of the settees.
She'd spent the night in the yellow and white bedroom that used to be hers as a child. No longer a
child, she hadn't belonged in it. No longer the woman
she used to be, she didn't belong in her apartment,
either. So where did she belong?

"You're up early, Gillian. You didn't sleep well?"

her grandmother questioned while maneuvering her wheelchair toward the table where the butler had placed warm croissants and coffee.

"Too much to think about."

"You look unhappy." She said nothing else as Charles appeared and poured coffee for both of them. Without a word said to him, he left the room swiftly. The cup and saucer in her hand, Felicia stirred her spoon slowly. "Don't think about Redmond anymore. He isn't worth your time, my dear."

"I wasn't thinking about him." Because she'd heard her grandmother's concern, she tried to act normal and uncurled to lean toward the coffee table where Charles had set her cup and saucer.

"Who then? Nicholas?" her grandmother suddenly questioned.

Ann met her deciphering gaze for only a second then averted her eyes. The croissants looked delicious, but she doubted she could eat.

"Oh, I see the problem," her grandmother said. "He does lead a life different from yours. You're used to so much more than he can give you."

Ann had never considered that a factor.

"Why do I get the impression there is more wrong?" Felicia asked.

"Nick knew that Redmond was seeing her and never told me."

"Oh." She set her spoon down. "Now I understand." Worry deepened the lines in her face. "I have to admit I'm guilty, also. I knew, too. He'd told me at the party that he'd learned a few hours earlier about

Redmond's association with that woman. He wanted to tell you.''

"But he didn't.''

"That was my fault. I thought he should wait until after the party. I can only hope you'll understand. You'd been through so much, and I knew how stressful the party was for you. You seemed so unhappy whenever Redmond was near. Believe me, my dear, no one intended to keep anything from you.'' Her frown deepened. "I had hoped you would be happy now. Now that you have your memory back. Now that you know who you are.''

"Gillian Somerset.'' Ann released a mirthless laugh. She knew her name and where she lived, but did she really know the woman who'd been engaged to Redmond? "Yes, I guess I do. But the person I am isn't so admirable. I'm a gullible, easily fooled woman.''

"Oh, my dear.'' Felicia sighed heavily. "You're loving and generous. Good traits. Wonderful ones to give to the right man.''

Ann echoed her words. "The right man.'' Funny how they'd come full circle to her problem.

"You told me you loved Nicholas. And he loves you?''

"He says he loves me.''

"Then what is wrong?''

Her throat tight, she felt as if her uncertainty might strangle her. "Can I believe him?''

"Trust yourself to know.''

But she didn't. She'd made so many mistakes. "How can I trust my own judgment?''

"Has he indicated that he's like Redmond?"

Every good quality Nick possessed, Redmond had lacked. "Hardly." She drew a hard breath at the truth in her own words.

Thoughtful, her grandmother remained quiet for a long moment. "So it isn't him that you don't trust?"

Slowly Ann raised her head to meet her grandmother's stare squarely. The truth had come in the form of another question. "No, it isn't," she answered softly.

One step into his house, and Nick knew no moments would be easy now. Ann's scent lingered on the air. Her bookmark, a piece of torn paper, marked her spot in a book. Her toothbrush occupied a place in the medicine cabinet. Restless, he ran a hand over the stubble on his jaw while he waited for water to fill the coffeepot. Damn Harper. How could a man not treasure her? She was special, caring, loving. Why would any man not value her? He'd seen examples of how money clouded thinking. The more some people had, the more they wanted. He'd always been satisfied with his life. He worked hard; he lived comfortably. He'd envisioned someday sharing what he had with a woman. Not just any woman. She had a name now. He knew the woman he wanted.

Tension tightening his neck, he fought the sense of unfamiliar helplessness that was engulfing him. Softly he swore while he plugged in the coffeemaker. Because others had treated her gentle heart so carelessly, he'd lost.

The hurting shadowed him. He missed her, felt desperate to hear her voice. So what could he do? This wasn't the same as it had been with Julia. Ann had loved him. At least, he thought she had. Oh damn, what did he know for sure? Possibly he'd let his own feelings make him believe more existed than really had.

He cursed out loud and started to leave the kitchen to find something to occupy his mind when he heard a distinct sound outside the back door. Muttering, he opened it. The cat meowed again. "Coming around during the day now? Suppose you think I'll keep feeding you?"

Nick left the door open and set a dish on the kitchen floor. With a look back, he stared at the cat. "Come on in," he murmured to it while pouring milk into the dish.

One paw and then another cautiously crossed the threshold.

"Come on. It's you and me now."

For a long moment, he leaned against the counter and watched the cat licking away at the milk. He, too, was a reminder.

Turning to pour another cup of coffee, Nick checked the clock and raked a hand through his hair. He couldn't sleep. He'd shower, go back to work. He'd exist. No, dammit, he'd... The thought died as the doorbell rang.

Annoyed, in no mood to see anyone, he downed a swallow of coffee, letting the person stew outside the door. As the bell rang persistently several times, grumbling, he ambled to the door. There should be a law against solicitors at eight in the morning. His mood foul, he flung open the front door.

An endless moment passed for Ann. He said nothing, waiting. Tired looking, in need of a shave, he simply stared at her. As one excruciating second of silence after another passed, nerves danced within her. The welcome mat wasn't out. Well, she really hadn't expected it. "May I come in?"

Even as the sight of her roused pleasure, Nick kept his fingers curled on the doorknob. She could rip him open if he let her. "Why?"

Ann agonized. What had she done to him last night? All she'd been thinking of then was saving herself from more heartache. Nerves close to the surface, she steadied herself with a long breath. From what she knew about Nick's marriage, he might have been wary, too. But he'd shown more courage. He'd taken a chance when he'd told her he loved her. He'd trusted and loved her enough to believe she wouldn't turn on him as Julia had. Courage. One of them had a lot more of it than the other. And that person hadn't been her.

"May I—" She saw the hurt in his eyes. Hurt she'd caused. Opening her hand, she pointed toward the living room. She'd have wished for more than a nod. Self-doubt skittered through her, sending a cowardly urge to flee, but the need to feel his arms around her proved greater. "Please don't be angry."

Nick deliberately kept furniture between them. What was this about? Gratitude?

"Nick, I'm sorry. I'm so sorry. I said I didn't know who I could trust. That wasn't the truth." Ann forced herself to sit on the sofa though she longed to step closer to him. "I have always trusted you."

Head bent, he recalled the disbelief that had flashed in her eyes last night, the accusation in her voice. "This time I guess you had good reason not to trust me. I let you down."

Ann straightened her back. She doubted she'd find another man who'd show such understanding to a woman who'd hurt him. "I'm sorry I hurt you. I acted like a fool."

"Did you?" he countered. "Or did I?"

Ann wanted to cry. He'd thought she was no better than Julia. "No, me," she insisted. She'd faced other difficult moments. She would handle these, too. Too much depended on her explaining what she'd felt. One more chance, she prayed. Give me one more chance. Sitting, she rested her hands in her lap and fiddled nervously with the strap of her purse. "Last night," she started, and stopped. "Last night so much happened. The memories that came back were difficult to understand. I didn't realize how much some of them had affected me."

Studying her closely, Nick rested his backside against the arm of a nearby chair. Who knew better than him how much burden she'd carried about the memories she might remember? What if they're sad ones, ones I want to forget, she'd once asked him.

With a helpless sigh, Ann rose from the sofa she'd just sat on. The warmth wasn't in his eyes, and she wondered if any explanation would bring it back. "Don't you understand?" she said with a touch of frustration. "It was never you I doubted. It was myself. I'd made so many mistakes that I was afraid to trust my own judgment." Ann stepped closer, yet he remained half sitting on the arm of the chair. "I can't say I'm sorry all of this happened. I've learned a lot about myself. I understand the woman I was, but I'm not sure I like her."

From day one, he'd admired her. Even before he'd fallen in love with her, he'd liked the way she could sit quietly, staring out the window. He'd liked the way her head tilted when questions formed in her mind. He liked her strength. "I always did."

Ann pressed her lips firmly together and swallowed hard as tears threatened. "Do you still?" she asked unsteadily.

His own vulnerability rocked him. She could strip him clean if he opened his arms to her, and she walked away again. "Do I like you?" he asked, not sure what she wanted him to say.

Moistening her lips, she wished to ease the tension between them. "Yes, and—" He'd told her he loved her, she reminded herself. She drew a hard, leveling breath. If you love, you trust. Well, she loved him. She had to trust him and believe he'd meant those words of love. "Do you still love me?" she whispered, moving a few more steps toward him. "Because I love you."

Nick ran a hand over his face. Those words could be his downfall again. Or—or he could find everything he wanted with the woman he loved, the one he needed in his life. "Is that what you came here to say?"

Uncertain, she heard a nervous edge in her voice. "There's more, but yes, that's what I came to say."

Showing the same toughness he'd always seen, she met his stare squarely as if ready to take a punch.

Her heart pounding, she inched closer. "If—if you still want me."

"If I still want you?" Nick asked in disbelief, stunned she'd even question that.

Anxiety swept out of her when he caught her at the waist and pulled her near to stand between his legs.

"I told you that I wanted to spend the rest of my life with you." His lips curved in a slow smile. "I love you. That didn't stop because we both were acting like idiots."

Relief swayed her into him. "Why didn't you say so right away?" she asked, coiling her arms around his neck, aching to feel the heat of him against her.

Nick couldn't help grinning. Lightly he caressed her lips with a fingertip. "Why didn't you?"

For the first time since she'd entered the house, she felt calmer. "Because you deserve more." As she leaned against the arm at her back, he captured her eyes with his steadfast stare. Truth. It was a part of what they were together. "I was hurt by Redmond, but there's so much to explain, Nick," Ann insisted. "Your memories are there for you to pick and choose, mine all came at me at once last night." The admission was accompanied by a sigh. "I didn't have a choice about what I remembered, and some of the memories were painful ones." Like a mother who'd had terrible mood swings and heard voices, a father who'd made promises and broken them. "I learned not to trust. That woman returned when my memory came back.''

Nick stroked her hair. ''You're also a strong woman. No one knows that better than me. I watched your bravery through times when other people would have folded.''

''But I've made my share of mistakes.''

''Who hasn't?''

''I meant what I said to you. All my doubts were here,'' she said, placing a hand to her chest.

Nick had gone through enough of his own pain because of rejection to relate to how it altered the way he viewed other people. Hadn't he dealt with his own doubts about Ann because of Julia? ''Are they gone now?''

Ann gave him a wry smile. ''I'm not sure all of them are, but I have none about you.''

The need to kiss her overwhelmed him, but he had to clear away all uncertainties. ''You know I can't give you everything you're used to.''

Watching his mouth, dying for his taste, Ann didn't even want to discuss such a thing. ''No, you gave me so much more than money will ever give me,'' she said, running a hand over the back of his head. She'd spoken honestly. He'd loved her without knowing who she was. He'd taught her to trust again.

''Does that mean you want to marry me?'' he questioned, gently brushing her hair back.

Laughing with the happiness bubbling inside her, she kissed him hard. ''Yes,'' she said, beneath his smiling lips. She'd once wondered why she'd lost her memory, why that had happened to her. Now she saw it as a blessing in disguise. During some muddled times, she'd learned about herself, some good and bad. She'd uncovered truth. Most of all, she'd found a man whose love she would never doubt. Her heart full of love, she savored the moment. All she'd wanted had been found during the most difficult days of her life. They'd also been the happiest. "Yes. Whenever you say." With her cheek pressed against his now, she released a short laugh at what she saw. Curled in a corner behind the chair, the cat contentedly licked a paw. "We seem to have a pet."

Nick drew in the scent that seemed so uniquely hers. "We always did."

"I knew you liked that cat," Ann teased, smiling back at him.

Nick kissed the tip of her nose. "And you."

As his hand roamed down her hip to her thigh, she couldn't recall ever feeling so certain about anything or anyone before. "There is one more thing."

Heat already stirred inside him. In fascination, he watched her lips form a slow, enticing smile. "What do you want?"

"You," she whispered.

On a rough laugh, Nick scooped her into his arms. "Anytime," he answered, before capturing her mouth beneath his.

* * * * *

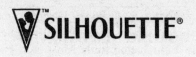

SILHOUETTE

⟩SPECIAL EDITION⟨®

COMING NEXT MONTH

WHAT TO DO ABOUT BABY Martha Hix

That's My Baby!
Caroline Grant's mother had had baby Natalie very late in life, which
was why her lawyer was now trying to persuade Caroline to 'inherit'
her toddler sister. And Kent Maxwell was very persuasive!

VALENTINE'S CHILD Natalie Bishop

Fifteen years ago Sherry Sterling and Jake Beckett made a child, a
child who now wanted to know her natural parents, which meant that
Sherry was going to have to visit Jake and tell him that he had a
daughter...

SUBSTITUTE BRIDE Trisha Alexander

Rachel just couldn't tell David, the man she'd secretly loved for years,
that her twin had left him at the altar. So she took her sister's place!

THAT WILD STALLION Shirley Larson

Rancher's son Travis McCallister had stoically rebuffed Elizabeth
Grant's girlish advances years ago, but now he was coming home.
Could she finally break through his resistance?

THE READY-MADE FAMILY Laurie Paige

Isadora Chavez fascinated tycoon Harrison Stone; in fact, he was losing
his head—until she blackmailed him into marriage! That meant he was
taking off the kid gloves. She would be his. *Or else.*

NOTHING SHORT OF A MIRACLE Patricia Thayer

Nick Malone didn't want to risk his son getting too attached to his
favourite nurse. For they'd already been abandoned by one woman
when the going got tough...

COMING NEXT MONTH FROM

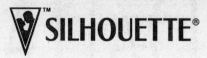

Intrigue
Danger, deception and desire

INTO THIN AIR Karen Leabo
THE DESPERADO Patricia Rosemoor
TWICE BURNED Pamela Burford
SWORN TO SILENCE Vickie York

Desire
*Provocative, sensual love stories for the
woman of today*

A MEMORABLE MAN Joan Hohl
TEXAS GLORY Joan Elliott Pickart
THE 7LB, 2OZ VALENTINE Marie Ferrarella
A CHILD OF HER OWN Beverly Barton
MARRY ME, COWBOY Peggy Moreland
HOW TO SUCCEED AT LOVE Susan Connell

Sensation
*A thrilling mix of passion, adventure
and drama*

THE 14TH...AND FOREVER Merline Lovelace
FATHER FIGURE Rebecca Daniels
A MAN WITHOUT LOVE Beverly Bird
IN MEMORY'S SHADOW Linda Randall Wisdom

NEW YEAR PARTY!

How would you like to win a year's supply of Silhouette® Books? Well you can and they're FREE! Simply complete the competition below and send it to us by 31st July 1998. The first five correct entries picked after the closing date will each win a year's subscription to the Silhouette series of their choice. What could be easier?

BALLOONS	BUFFET	ENTERTAIN
STREAMER	DANCING	INVITE
DRINKS	CELEBRATE	FANCY DRESS
MUSIC	PARTIES	HANGOVER

Please turn over for details of how to enter...

C8A

HOW TO ENTER

Can you find our twelve party words? They're all hidden somewhere in the grid. They can be read backwards, forwards, up, down or diagonally. As you find each word in the grid put a line through it. When you have completed your wordsearch, don't forget to fill in the coupon below, pop this page into an envelope and post it today—you don't even need a stamp!

**Silhouette New Year Party! Competition
FREEPOST CN81, Croydon, Surrey, CR9 3WZ**
EIRE readers send competition to PO Box 4546, Dublin 24.

Please tick the series you would like to receive if you are one of the lucky winners

Sensation™ ❑   Intrigue™ ❑   Desire™ ✓   Special Edition™ ❑

Are you a Reader Service™ Subscriber?   Yes ❑   No ✓

Mrs/Ms/Miss/Mr ...MISS... Intials ...H...
(BLOCK CAPITALS PLEASE)
Surname ...DICKINSON...

Address ...BROCKSTONES...
...KENTMERE, NR KENDAL...
...CUMBRIA... Postcode ...LA8 9JW...

(I am over 18 years of age)   C8A

One application per household. Competition open to residents of the UK and Ireland only. You may be mailed with offers from other reputable companies as a result of this application. If you would prefer not to receive such offers, please tick box. ❑

Closing date for entries is 31st July 1998.

Silhouette® is a registered trademark of Harlequin Enterprises used under licence by Harlequin Mills & Boon Limited.